Murder at the palace has the kingdom in an uproar! A little boy hasn't spoken since that terrible night. Mysterious undercurrents sweep through Montebello, as the boy's regal father falls for a nanny in disguise....

Meet the major players in this royal mystery:

Sir Dominic Chiara, M.D.: This doctor and knight in rusty armor will open his mind— and his heart—to help his son.

Sarah Hunter: She traveled halfway around the world to help a child. Now the boy and his father are threatening the well-planned order of her life.

Leo Chiara: What secret is locked away in this sweet little boy's mind?

Lady Honoria Satherwaite: Sir Dominic's irrepressible aunt is not above pulling a trick or two to get her way, especially in the interest of opening her nephew's eyes to love.

King Marcus Sebastiani: With his own son, Crown Prince Lucas Sebastiani, home at last, the king wishes the same joy for all his subjects. Sometimes, that can be royally arranged....

Estella and Bruno: Leo's former nanny and her beau have kept secrets from Estella's father...and from Sir Dominic.

Dear Reader,

Once again, Silhouette Intimate Moments starts its month off with a bang, thanks to Beverly Barton's *The Princess's Bodyguard*, another in this author's enormously popular miniseries THE PROTECTORS. A princess used to royal suitors has to "settle" for an in-name-only marriage to her commoner bodyguard. Or maybe she isn't settling at all? Look for more Protectors in *On Her Guard*, Beverly Barton's Single Title, coming next month.

ROMANCING THE CROWN continues with *Sarah's Knight* by Mary McBride. An arrogant palace doctor finds he needs help himself when his little boy stops speaking. To the rescue: a beautiful nanny sent to work with the child—but who winds up falling for the good doctor himself. And in Candace Irvin's *Crossing the Line*, an army pilot crash-lands, and she and her surviving passenger—a handsome captain—deal simultaneously with their attraction to each other and the ongoing crash investigation. Virginia Kantra begins her TROUBLE IN EDEN miniseries with *All a Man Can Do*, in which a police chief finds himself drawn to the reporter who is the sister of a prime murder suspect. In *The Cop Next Door* by Jenna Mills, a woman back in town to unlock the secrets of her past runs smack into the stubborn town sheriff. And Melissa James makes her debut with *Her Galahad*, in which a woman who thought her first husband was dead finds herself on the run from her abusive *second* husband. And who should come to her rescue but Husband Number One—not so dead after all!

Enjoy, and be sure to come back next month for more of the excitement and passion, right here in Intimate Moments.

Leslie J. Wainger
Executive Senior Editor

Please address questions and book requests to:
Silhouette Reader Service
U.S.: 3010 Walden Ave., P.O. Box 1325, Buffalo, NY 14269
Canadian: P.O. Box 609, Fort Erie, Ont. L2A 5X3

Sarah's Knight
MARY McBRIDE

INTIMATE MOMENTS™

Published by Silhouette Books

America's Publisher of Contemporary Romance

Special thanks and acknowledgment are given
to Mary McBride for her contribution
to the ROMANCING THE CROWN series.

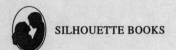 **SILHOUETTE BOOKS**

ISBN 0-373-27248-0

SARAH'S KNIGHT

Visit Silhouette at www.eHarlequin.com

Printed in U.S.A.

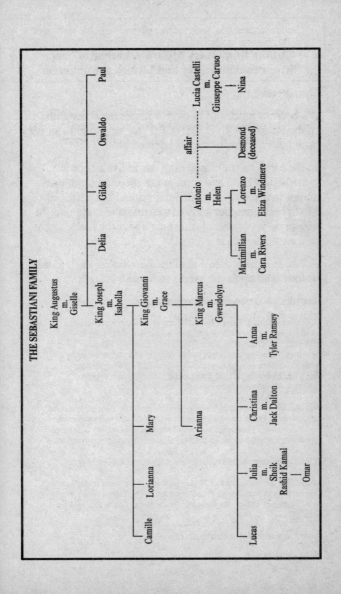

THE SEBASTIANI FAMILY

King Augustus
m.
Giselle

King Joseph   Delia   Gilda   Oswaldo   Paul
m.
Isabella

Camille   Lorianna   Mary

King Giovanni
m.
Grace

Arianna

King Marcus   Antonio   Lucia Castelli
m.   m.   m.
Gwendolyn   Helen   Giuseppe Caruso

Lucas   Julia   Christina   Anna   Nina
          m.   m.   m.
          Sheik   Jack Dalton   Tyler Ramsey
          Rashid Kamal

          Omar

affair

Maximillian   Lorenzo   Desmond
m.   m.   (deceased)
Cara Rivers   Eliza Windmere

A note from Mary McBride, author of over fifteen contemporary and historical romances:

Dear Reader,

It's been so much fun to work with all the other authors of the ROMANCING THE CROWN series, and I'm very proud to be a part of such a talented group.

In the early stages of planning our individual books, e-mails flew back and forth at the speed of light, one author needing to confirm details about the palace in Montebello, another author inquiring about the interior of a royal jet or one of us asking about the landscaping of a particular place.

I've been having a ball reading these books each month as they lead up to the events in *Sarah's Knight*.

Thanks so much for coming along with us on this wonderful, international trip!

All the best,

Mary McBride

Prologue

The ringing phone sliced through Dr. Elliot Hunter's sleep like a scalpel.

Okay. Okay.

What time was it? Where the hell was he anyway? He opened one eye and saw a thin blade of daylight between drawn curtains—the resonant golden daylight that was peculiar to San Francisco in early autumn.

He was home. Thank God. The clock read 1:15 p.m., so he must've slept more than ten hours, but it seemed he'd only dropped into bed an hour or two ago after a sixteen-hour flight on a Royal Montebellan jet from Cairo, too exhausted and jet-lagged to even make love to his beautiful wife. He stretched out his left arm now, encountering only cool and empty sheets. No Kate. She would've left for the clinic hours before.

It'd be nice, he thought blearily, if she were calling him now, suggesting a lunchtime tryst. He snatched the phone from its cradle and grunted "Hunter" only to be greeted with a dial tone and another shrill, insistent ring. More awake now, Elliot realized it was the other phone on the bedside table. The secure phone. The one restricted for communication between the Noble Men.

Christ. He'd just spent eight days in the Middle East trying to cool tempers and to put out some of the fires forever being sparked in that volatile region. What more could he do?

"Hunter," he growled into the second phone.

"How was your vacation?"

There was no mistaking his father's voice—tough as his wiry physique, tinged with his keen sense of humor. When Dr. Gordon Hunter had worked as a field surgeon in Vietnam—Captain Hunter, then—his mobile operating room had no doubt born a startling resemblance to the one in *M*A*S*H*. His father, in his late sixties now, was the best man Elliot knew, a belief he had made official when he'd asked his old man to stand up for him when he and Dr. Katherine Remson were married last year.

"The vacation was great," Elliot replied. "Thanks. I did some snorkeling."

He knew that his father would translate his words to mean that he had successfully and secretly entered

Cyprus at Famagusta, where he represented the Noble Men in negotiations between Greece and Tamir.

"Was it pleasant?" his father asked.

"Only slightly," Elliot said.

"Ah, well." It was one of the few times the young surgeon detected weariness and worry in the elder doctor's voice. "I wanted to let you know I just put your sister on a plane to visit our old friend."

Elliot sat straight up in bed. "You what?" Our old friend was the commonly used code name for King Marcus of Montebello. Why the hell was Dad sending Sarah to Montebello?

"Marc has a young friend in need of her expertise," his father said, abandoning the standard, veiled communication, which wasn't like him at all, even in light of the secure phone.

Now Elliot was fully alert. Worried, too. He swung his legs over the side of the bed as he spoke. "They have child psychologists in San Sebastian, Dad. Why send Sarah halfway across the planet? What's up?"

Gordon Hunter sighed. "She got herself engaged while you were away. To that idiot accountant who works for Kate's clinic."

Elliot blinked. "Warren?"

He took his father's gruff curse for a yes, then sat there rubbing the stubble on his jaw, doubly confused. As far as Elliot knew, his twenty-nine-year-old sister wasn't interested in marriage in any way, shape or form. And even assuming she *was* interested, why in the world would a woman as beautiful and vibrant and free-spirited as Sarah Hunter choose Warren Dill for a mate? The guy was completely humorless, an accountant to the marrow of his bones. His idea of a good time was probably knocking back a few lite beers while he read actuarial tables.

"Why?" It was the only question Elliot could think to ask.

"Your guess is as good as mine, but apparently her mind's made up. She's like your mother in that respect, you know." His father sighed. "Stubborn. Mulish."

Elliot almost laughed. Gordon Hunter wasn't exactly known for his fickleness or ability to be swayed once he'd made up his mind. He was a stubborn, diehard ally and a formidable foe. Sarah hadn't fallen far from the tree. "So you shipped her off to Montebello, hoping she'll come to her senses," he said. "It would've been cheaper to send her to London, Dad, or on a Caribbean cruise. Safer, too. Things are still pretty unsettled in Montebello. I heard there was a murder on the palace grounds."

"Yes, Marc mentioned that. The victim, Desmond Caruso, was his nephew. Rather a ne'er-do-well, I gather. Coincidentally, the child who needs psychological help stopped speaking at about the same time as the murder. You might know his father, Elliot. Sir Dominic Chiara is the palace physician."

"I know him by reputation." What Elliot had heard was that Dr. Chiara's promising career as a surgeon had been derailed by the death of his wife. Hell, they'd probably had a lot in common a few years ago. On the other hand, maybe not. Dominic, or Nick as he was known to friends, Chiara had been left with a baby son. Elliot had been left with no one when his wife and baby daughter died. "I didn't meet him. He was away on sabbatical when Katie and I were there last year after the bombing."

His father snorted. "Well, he's there now, and apparently in severe denial about his son's problem these past few weeks. At least according to the king. Marc's hoping Sarah can set the fellow straight."

"Knowing my little sister, she'll accomplish that in about two minutes."

"The hope, my boy, is that it will take her a bit longer than two minutes. At least long enough to forget about this ridiculous engagement."

Elliot laughed. "Careful, Dad. You're playing Cupid again."

"I'm damned good at it, too. Look at you and Kate."

The playfulness evaporated from Gordon Hunter's voice then. He was a Noble Man again, through and through, when he said, "Stop by the house this evening, Elliot. We'll discuss that snorkeling."

Chapter 1

Somewhere high above the Mediterranean, Sarah Hunter stared at her watch, which was still set on Pacific time. So was her body clock, she thought, and since it was after 11:00 p.m. at home in San Francisco, it came as little surprise that she could hardly keep her eyes open. No surprise, either, that she couldn't for the life of her figure out what the local time would be when she finally—finally!—landed in Montebello.

Warren would know. Her fiancé was a marvel when it came to numbers of any kind—time zones, mileage, cost per page of copying patient files at the clinic, square yardage for the new Berber carpet in her apartment—including closets, everything. If it had anything to do with numbers, Warren Dill had it covered. What a guy.

Sarah hadn't even had a chance to tell poor Warren goodbye this afternoon. Her father had hustled her to the airport and onto King Marcus Sebastiani's private Gulfstream jet, conveniently available after Elliot's return, so fast her head was practically spinning.

Just about the last thing she'd said to her father was "Call Warren and explain where I've gone and why, will you, Dad? Tell him I'll be in touch as soon as possible."

But when he gave her a thumb's up and replied "Absolutely," Sarah noticed that furtive little glint in his eyes, the same glint she'd witnessed for her entire life when her father would say he'd been "away on business." Dr. Gordon Hunter was as chock-full of secrets today as he had been for the past several decades. Bless his devious heart, he thought she didn't have a clue about his international, often heroic activities with the Noble Men, but Sarah wasn't stupid. Years ago she'd learned the secret from her mother. She was incredibly proud of her father and his efforts in keeping the world on an even keel.

That didn't keep her from being aggravated with him, though. At the airport, when she'd handed him a hastily scribbled list of Warren's numbers—office, home, cell phone and pager—Sarah couldn't help but notice that old Gordo crumpled the paper in his big fist before he shoved it in a back pocket.

Okay. Fine. Her supermacho father didn't like wimpy Warren. Sometimes Sarah didn't like him very much either. But she was still going to marry him, dammit. She'd be wearing an engagement ring right now if it weren't for the fact that she never wore jewelry—it distracted her young patients too much— and the fact that Warren considered diamonds a terrible investment when, for the same price as a one-karat, pear-shaped solitaire, he could buy her a hundred shares of Microsoft.

So what if it wasn't a marriage of the heart? As a psychotherapist, she gave far more credence to the mind and its rational choices. She'd chosen Warren after great deliberation. They wanted the same things in life—a perfect balance of home and family and career, and they were equally determined to achieve their mutual desires. Sarah didn't have a doubt in the world that they would.

"We shall be landing in approximately forty-five minutes, Signorina Hunter."

Giorgio, the wickedly handsome flight attendant and for the past fourteen hours or so her own personal slave, materialized out of nowhere. How in the world did he manage to look as if he'd had a good night's sleep? His black uniform with the gold braid on the sleeves was as perfectly pressed as it had been hours ago in San Francisco when she'd boarded the plane.

"May I serve you a small snack, signorina?" he crooned in his deep and dreamy Italian-accented English. "Strawberries and cream, perhaps? Royal Tamir figs for the lovely lady? Caviar? Or an omelet, if you prefer something more substantial?"

During the long flight, he'd not only been plying her with gourmet goodies—champagne in crystal flutes, Beluga caviar, and to-die-for Godiva chocolates imprinted with the royal Sebastiani crest—but they'd been flirting with each other pretty outrageously.

Sarah imagined that was part of Giorgio's job description. "Make the lady passengers happy." As for herself, well, she was just naturally flirtatious, it had nothing to do with her attachment to Warren, and it was a pleasant way to pass the hours over the Continental Divide, the Great Plains, the Atlantic, and at last the Mediterranean. It was all perfectly harmless. She was, after all, engaged to Warren, and she suspected gorgeous Giorgio spent his layovers with an equally gorgeous significant other named Carlo or Leonardo or Fabrizio.

Still, his compliments were helping her brush up on her Italian, a language she knew only peripherally from being fluent in Spanish. Let's see. According to Giorgio, she had *graziosi verdi occhi,* which meant he thought her green eyes were lovely. Her shoulder length hair was *colore marrone ed ondulati*. Actually, she liked to think of her brown hair as wavy, not undulating. That sounded a bit too much like Medusa. As for the rest of her, Giorgio hadn't so much described her in words, but rather with a lift of his eyebrows that implied she was fairly well endowed. *Zaftig* was no doubt the same in any language.

She smiled up at him now, a full, flirtatious two hundred watts, and batted her *graziosi verdi occhi*. "I just can't bear to think of life without you, Giorgio."

"I am flattered, signorina." He grinned, which made him look like a direct descendant of Apollo. "Does that mean the signorina would like the strawberries and cream?"

"You read my mind," Sarah said with a laugh.

After she had consumed the perfect red berries and the thick cream served in a small porcelain bowl featuring the black and gold royal crest of the House of Sebastiani, Sarah visited the royal lavatory, a paradise of black marble and solid gold fixtures, where she attempted to make repairs to her sleep-deprived, nonroyal face. Luckily, her undulating hair only required a quick swipe of a comb and a swing of her head to fall into place.

After she brushed her teeth with a royally monogrammed toothbrush and the royal Colgate tartar control, she returned to her seat—actually it was an enormous buttery leather club chair—and fastened her seat belt in preparation for landing.

"Look down there, signorina." Giorgio angled a lean hip onto the arm of her seat and pointed toward the window just as the plane banked to the right. "Montebello. She is beautiful, is she not?"

Beautiful, even in Giorgio's sexily accented Italian, didn't come anywhere near describing the island kingdom below. Montebello rose out of the turquoise Mediterranean like a rough jewel. Its central mountains, green and glorious, sloped to bright blue coves and wide white beaches. High above one of those beaches, the capital city of San Sebastian hugged the mountainside and glittered in the morning sun.

And somewhere down there, Sarah thought, was a troubled little boy in need of her help. Suddenly she wasn't quite so tired anymore. She was ready to go to work.

Half an hour later, when the royal limousine rolled to a stop on the cobbled drive in front of the palace, Sarah drew in a deep and calming breath.

Okay. Just breathe. Settle down. Don't even think of it as a palace, she told herself. Think of it as the home of one of your father's oldest and dearest friends. That's all.

Oh, right. The fact that her father's oldest and dearest friend was the monarch of a Mediterranean kingdom was a minor detail. And his home, the building looming outside the limo's window, was just your everyday marble-columned, fifty- or sixty-room palatial residence with armed, uniformed guards standing sentry at the front entrance.

The stone-faced chauffeur opened the door for her and held out a gray-gloved hand. "Signorina."

Sarah was the sort of person who never rode even a few blocks in a taxi without learning the name of the cabbie, along with the names of his wife and children, their hopes and dreams, their peccadilloes and political affiliations. People were naturally drawn to her, as she was to them. And it was her business, too—knowing people, children mostly. Listening to them. Drawing them out. But in the royal stretch limo there hadn't been a chance to chat or listen because the driver had sat about a quarter mile ahead of her, separated by several layers of dark velvet curtains and multiple panes of glass.

It was all so official. So—so damn royal. Regal beyond belief. She wasn't the sort of person who was easily rattled, but now there was a definite tremor in her hand as she placed it in the waiting gray glove.

"Gracias," she said, using Spanish rather than Italian in her agitated state, cursing herself for this uncharacteristic case of nerves. It wasn't like her at all.

Much to her relief, the chauffeur cracked the tiniest of smiles before he murmured *"De nada,* señorita," in sympathetic Spanish.

"Welcome, Miss Hunter."

The greeting came from a woman who was descending the broad marble steps in front of the palace. She was slim and elegant, the picture of sleek organization in an exquisitely tailored navy suit. Her dark hair was pulled back in a severe bun and a pair of tortoiseshell glasses were perched on her nose. She was probably Sarah's age—just shy of the big Three-O—but gave the impression of being much older, not to mention far more sophisticated, or at least better put together. "Welcome to Montebello," she said in a voice that was more official than friendly.

"Thank you," Sarah replied.

"I am Sophia Strezzi, the royal appointment secretary," the woman said briskly, her accent in that vague Continental range, somewhere between British and Italian and French, but elegant nonetheless. She grasped Sarah's hand in a firm, dry, perfunctory shake. "The king's personal secretary, Albert, asked me to greet you. I trust you had a pleasant flight."

"Yes, I did. Very pleasant."

Sarah was about to pass along a few words of praise for gorgeous Giorgio and the rest of the crew who'd taken such good care of her, but Sophia Strezzi was clearly finished discussing the flight. She dropped Sarah's hand like a hot potato and began snapping directions at the chauffeur.

Temporarily forgotten, Sarah took that moment to

gaze around the palace grounds, the centerpiece of which appeared to be an enormous and magnificent marble fountain. There were bright rainbows in the cascading water, and the surrounding landscape was lush, a brilliant sunlit green. Beneath the tall and stately royal palm trees, the grounds nearly exploded in colorful hibiscus and oleander and other flowering shrubs. There were geraniums spilling from huge pots in colors that Sarah had never seen before. Crimson and cardinal and sizzling pink.

All around her, the air was warm and exotically perfumed. No wonder her parents had bought property in Montebello for their eventual retirement. No wonder her brother, Elliot, and her best friend, Katherine Remson, had fallen in love here last year. It was paradise. Absolute paradise.

"Your luggage will be taken to Sir Dominic's residence," Sophia said, and before Sarah could even blink or ask why, the woman continued, "And now, if you'll follow me, Miss Hunter." She swiveled on her polished black pumps and headed toward the grand entrance of the palace with Sarah tagging along behind.

At the main door, a uniformed guard held up a hand and murmured, "*Scusa,* signorina" as he slowly passed some sort of metal detector up and down the length of her.

While she was being screened, Sarah couldn't help but notice that Sophia Strezzi was also giving her a fairly thorough once-over with her dark brown eyes. Judging from the woman's taut mouth and pinched expression, Sarah assumed she hadn't passed the inspection with flying colors. Well, if her father hadn't rushed her so this morning, she might have worn something a little spiffier than black linen slacks and a plain, rather mannish white cotton blouse. She probably looked as wrinkled as a shar-pei puppy and not half as adorable. Certainly not fit to meet a king.

"I wonder if I could change clothes and freshen up a little before—"

Sophia cut her off with a brusque wave of her hand. "That won't be possible. It's half past eleven already. The king is expecting you."

"Oh." Looking at her watch, Sarah stifled a groan, not to mention a yawn. Actually it was half past midnight in San Francisco as well as on Sarah's body clock, but the royal appointment secretary didn't seem to recognize any time zones or itineraries other than her own.

At least she didn't set off any security bells, Sarah thought, as she followed the woman into the huge marble floored reception hall of the palace.

"This is magnificent," she murmured, gazing around her at all the gleaming marble, the gold-and-crystal chandeliers, the huge royal portraits in gilded frames, dozens of flags in stanchions and more uniformed guards standing sober post.

"Yes," Sophia tossed over her shoulder. "Perhaps

there will be time for a tour after your appointment with the king.''

If she wasn't too tired to put one foot in front of the other, Sarah thought, continuing in Sophia's wake around the grand staircase and down a long, wide corridor lined with huge potted palms and more royal portraits in gilded frames.

''This is the solarium,'' Sophia said at last, opening a door and gesturing Sarah ahead of her. ''I'll inform His Highness of your arrival. He'll be with you in a moment. Please make yourself comfortable, Miss Hunter.''

Comfortable. Oh, sure. That was obviously a palace joke.

To truly make herself comfortable, Sarah would've had to put on a pair of old gray sweats and her pink bunny slippers! But her nerves settled down a bit when she realized Sophia hadn't ushered her into a gilded formal throne room, but rather a lovely, glassed-in sitting room with gold-and-cream-colored upholstered furniture that actually looked inviting and appeared to be used on a regular basis. There were magazines on a glass coffee table and there was even a big screen TV peeking out from a discrete entertainment center. If Sarah lived here, this would definitely be the room where she'd hang out.

''The view is spectacular, no?'' Sophia pointed toward the wall of windows where in the distance the brilliant blue sky met the azure, sun-kissed sea.

"Quite spectacular," Sarah agreed. Much as she loved San Francisco and its breathtaking views, she had to admit her hometown paled in comparison to San Sebastian. "Have you always lived in Montebello?" she asked.

"Yes. Always."

The woman's reply was cool and rather curt, leading Sarah to believe that Sophia Strezzi didn't like her very much. She wondered what she could possibly have done in a mere five minutes to alienate the woman so. Usually people warmed to her instantly. Her parents hadn't nicknamed her Sunshine for nothing. Even Warren, who didn't have much of a sense of humor, occasionally called her Miss Congeniality. But it seemed it would take more than Sarah's natural warmth and sunshine to melt a human ice carving like Sophia.

"May I offer you something while you wait?" the appointment secretary asked on her way to the door. "Tea? Or perhaps you prefer coffee?"

At the moment, a couple fingers of Jack Daniel's on the rocks didn't sound all that bad. She wondered bleakly if the palace bar was open this early in the day even as she replied, "Nothing, thank you," and wandered toward the wide windows. "I'll just savor the view."

"Very well. After your appointment, I'll show you to Sir Dominic's residence."

If the woman hadn't seemed in such a rush to escape, Sarah might have asked her about Sir Dominic Chiara. Especially the ''sir'' business. What was that all about? Was he royalty, too? A duke or a baron or some sort of grand poobah?

Her father hadn't had time to explain much—only that Sir Dominic was the palace physician and that his five-year-old son, Leo, had stopped speaking several weeks ago. According to Gordon Hunter, the king was far more concerned about the boy's condition than his own father was. But that didn't strike her as so strange or unusual. Physicians were renowned for ignoring illness and disabilities in their own families. It had something to do with their God complex, Sarah had decided.

Still, to ignore sudden muteness in such a little boy was rather extreme, even for a godlike physician. Somehow she pictured Sir Dominic as an older man, her father's age perhaps. Maybe he was simply too old to mount a great deal of concern for a child he'd had so late in life. She wondered how much Sophia knew about the relationship between Dr. Chiara and his son.

''Ms. Strezzi, if I could just ask you…''

Too late. The solarium door was just closing on the secretary's stiff shoulder blades. With a sigh, Sarah turned back to the window, reminding herself that her own ruffled and anxious feelings were unimportant right now. The only feelings that were important at the moment were those of the little boy who'd gone suddenly and quite inexplicably silent.

In her practice as a psychologist at her sister-in-law's clinic in San Francisco, she'd worked with two cases of selective mutism, but neither child had exhibited symptoms suddenly after years of normal speech. Both children had had language problems, not to mention various behavior problems, from infancy.

Dr. Chiara's son, on the other hand, had apparently talked a proverbial blue streak until several weeks ago, when he stopped speaking completely. That sudden onset suggested trauma to Sarah. There was still so much she didn't know.

Her gaze drifted across the lovely blue sea where a cruise ship slowly nosed into a pier. For a moment she wished she were here in Montebello under different circumstances. She wished she were a happy vacationer rather than a working psychologist. Someone footloose and fancy-free. A honeymooner, perhaps.

The thought made Sarah roll her eyes in exasperation. She wasn't going to have a honeymoon, was she? Warren—utterly practical Warren—had already determined that a hefty down payment on a house was far smarter than pouring money into a frivolous trip. He'd used that word. Frivolous. Well, maybe so, but...

For someone who loved to travel, she really hadn't

done all that much of it. Not lately, anyway. When she was young there had been wonderful family excursions with her mother and father and big brother, Elliot, to the national parks and treasures of the U.S.A. Yosemite. Yellowstone. Crater Lake. The Grand Canyon. The Great Smoky Mountains. The Ozarks. The Everglades.

When she was in high school, her father often would pull her out of Friday classes to attend weekend medical conferences with him in cities across the country. She'd been whisked away to all the major attractions and through all the major museums in the country. One summer in college she'd backpacked through Europe for three lovely months, but that seemed like a million years ago now.

And then, of course, after college, there had been her two-year stint in El Salvador with the Peace Corps, but she'd been anything but a carefree tourist there. Time off was rare while she was helping to set up a mental health clinic in Zacatecoluca. When she wasn't conducting workshops or teaching women to read or laying bricks, she was catching up on sleep.

Just once she'd like to go somewhere as a carefree spirit, with no one to tend to, with no obligations or agendas, with nothing more to do than laze on a sunstruck beach and float in turquoise seas.

Just once...

"Ah, Sarah. Daughter of my dear friend. Welcome. Welcome to Montebello."

Hearing the deep, melodious voice at her back, Sarah turned with a startled little gasp to see King Marcus Sebastiani, the ruler of Montebello. She hadn't anticipated that his entrance would be accompanied by a trumpet fanfare exactly, but she hadn't expected His Highness to sneak up on her, either. In her surprise, Sarah managed a clumsy curtsey. Actually two of them. Two and a half. Jeez. She probably looked more like a bobble-headed doll than a respectful visitor.

The king extended his hand. He was a tall, ruggedly handsome man in a dark business suit. His hair was thick and perfectly white. His kind eyes were twinkling, as if he were accustomed to people making complete fools out of themselves in his presence, and his smile was as warm as the Montebello sunshine that flooded the room.

"No need for formalities, my dear," he said. "Tell me, how is your father? He sounded well when I spoke to him yesterday. And your lovely mother?"

"They're both fine, sir. They send their very best. My brother, Elliot, as well."

"I'm indebted to your brother and Dr. Remson for their service at our hospital last year. The newlyweds are doing well, I presume?"

Sarah smiled, thinking how Dr. Katherine Remson Hunter no longer arrived at the clinic at the crack of dawn as she had before she and El were married. These days she was more likely to arrive half an hour late, with a very satisfied, thoroughly sated expression on her face. "Quite well. They're deliriously happy."

"Good. Good." King Marcus gestured toward a chair. "Please have a seat, Sarah, my dear."

The man put her at ease immediately, bless his royal heart, and soon Sarah almost forgot she was in the presence of a monarch as they chatted about her family and the stunning view through the windows. The king had a wonderful, deep-throated laugh that reminded her more than a little of her father's. After a while, though, his face changed from sunny to somber, as he leaned forward in his chair, sighed deeply and said, "The queen and I are extremely grateful for your help, Sarah. We're both quite fond of Sir Dominic and his little son, Leo. Quite worried, too."

Sarah nodded solemnly. It was time to go to work. "The child isn't speaking at all?" she asked.

King Marcus shook his head. "No. Not to my knowledge. Not a word in the past few weeks."

"Does his father have any idea of an event that might have set this off?"

"His father refuses to speak about young Leo's condition." The king scowled. "The man has his own case of muteness, it would seem. The stubborn donkey."

Sarah was thinking the same thing herself about Sir Dominic, only the word in her mind was a bit more crude than "donkey." The more the king disclosed to her about the man, the less she liked the palace physician.

His wife—young and very beautiful, according to the king—had been diagnosed with a virulent form of leukemia when she was newly pregnant. But because she'd wanted to give her husband a child so badly, the woman had kept her condition a secret and had refused the treatments that might have saved her life. Once the baby was born, once the young mother's illness was disclosed, it had been too late for chemotherapy to have much effect on her condition, and she had died when Leo was just a few months old.

Dr. Chiara had apparently been inconsolable. But in the traditional way of physicians and workaholics, he'd poured himself and his sorrows into his work, leaving the motherless child to the care of assorted housekeepers and nannies.

"All in all, though, the child seemed happy enough," said the king. "He was a little chatterbox, always talking. And then…" He shrugged. "We're all at a loss, I must say."

"I'll do my very best to help," Sarah told him. "I'd like to see Leo as soon as possible. I'd also like to interview his father and anyone who's been closely associated with him. An impartial observer can often find clues where none seem apparent to those directly related or involved."

She prided herself on her listening skills, which

had often succeeded in zeroing in on overlooked problems.

"In fact, the sooner I could interview Dr. Chiara, the better it will be. Is he available this afternoon?"

The king shifted rather uncomfortably in his chair, leading Sarah to believe that she'd just crossed an invisible line or breached royal protocol somehow. Uh-oh. Was she being too forward? Too aggressive? Not deferential enough? She didn't have a clue.

"I'm sorry, Your Majesty," she said, and then she almost laughed at the idea of addressing someone as "Your Majesty." It seemed so...so medieval. "I probably ought to have a royal rule book or something so I don't make a complete fool of myself while I'm here. It's just that sometimes I get carried away, a bit too eager to solve my patients' problems."

"Nonsense, my dear." He reached out to pat her hand. "There's no such thing as too much enthusiasm, especially in a worthy cause. You remind me very much of your father in that respect. Unfortunately..."

With a sigh, he sat back in his chair.

"...I'm afraid you're going to have to keep that professional enthusiasm of yours under wraps for a while."

"I don't understand."

He steepled his fingers beneath his chin as he continued. "My staff has arranged for you to move into

Sir Dominic's residence in the capacity of nanny to young Leo. It's a ruse, quite obviously. But one which will guarantee your access to the child. Otherwise..."

Ah. Sarah was beginning to see the light. "Otherwise his arrogant father will prevent me from seeing him," she finished for him.

"Well, yes. You might put it that way. As I said, Nick is being quite obstinate about this situation. The donkey."

She gave a tiny snort. "If you'll forgive the expression, Your Majesty, I'd say he's behaving like the part of the donkey that goes through the gate last."

"Indeed." The king smiled as if in complete agreement. "Perhaps you'll be able to apply a sound kick to that part of his anatomy, my dear."

Sarah sighed. She was a psychologist, and a damned good one. But she was accustomed to seeing children in a professional setting where her contact was usually limited to the traditional fifty-minute hour.

She certainly didn't know the first thing about nannying. Her sole experience with that profession had been the movie *Mary Poppins,* and the only part of the movie she had liked, other than the flying, of course, was the song "Supercalifragilisticexpialedocious."

The only thing Sarah was sure of at the moment

was that a little boy desperately needed her help in order to escape from his self-imposed prison of silence.

"I'll give it my best shot, Your Majesty." She grinned. "The child's problem as well as the father's behind."

Chapter 2

Sir Dominic Chiara stood at the window of his sixth-floor office in King Augustus Hospital, staring across the placid blue lake on the hospital grounds toward the palace in the distance. Wearing his starched white lab coat, with his stethoscope draped loosely about his neck, to the casual observer Dr. Chiara looked like a man in calm and quiet contemplation of a problem.

His arms were crossed. His head was slightly, almost thoughtfully cocked to the right. A frown dug deeply in between his dark eyebrows, and his finely carved mouth turned down at the corners. To all appearances, he was a physician caught up in thought, perhaps about the current, grave condition of a patient, perhaps about an upcoming, particularly difficult surgery, or about revelations in a recent medical journal he had read.

Actually, Nick Chiara was hiding out.

From Dr. Alex Bettancourt, the hospital's new chief of staff, who was no doubt this very moment foaming at the mouth while reading Dr. Chiara's letter in which he firmly announced, rather than humbly requested, a month-long leave of absence from all hospital duties. Beginning this afternoon. Right now, to be precise. He'd made all the proper arrangements. He'd made absolutely certain that no one, especially no one in the royal family, would be deprived of medical care in his absence. Nothing was negotiable.

From Dr. Antonia Solano, the venerable head of Ob-Gyn, who seemed to take his status as a widower as some sort of personal affront not only to herself but to every unmarried female on the hospital staff, as well. The woman was a certified nuisance. A terrible, albeit well-meaning, pest. She'd been nagging him incessantly for the past four years. He never passed her in the cafeteria or in a corridor that she didn't cluck her tongue and mutter ''Such a waste.'' Lately she'd taken more drastic measures, which included sending him articles copied from arcane medical journals decrying prolonged celibacy. As if he wasn't well acquainted with those.

And last but hardly least, he was in his office hiding out from the latest crop of giggling teenage volunteers from Santa Cecelia's Academy, those starry-eyed young girls in their candy-striped uniforms and crisp white caps, who insisted on mistaking him for some doctor on a popular American television program. George Somebody. His secretary, Paula, thought it was hysterical. Dammit.

"You do bear an uncanny resemblance to him, Dr. Chiara," she kept telling him. "Surely you've seen the show. It's extremely popular. Although Dr. Ross, the one you look like, isn't on it anymore. He moved to Oregon or something after fathering twins."

Nick sighed out loud now as he stared out the window. It didn't sound so bad, actually. Not fathering twins, God forbid, but moving halfway across the world to Oregon. If he remembered his geography properly, the state was on the Pacific coast in the northwest of the United States. With a rugged coastline and mountains and a relatively temperate climate, it wouldn't be so different from Montebello. Language certainly wouldn't present a problem there. He and his son, Leo, both spoke English equally as well as they spoke Italian.

Well, when Leo was speaking...

Nick closed his eyes, blotting out not only the view but the thought of his son's inexplicable muteness these past few weeks.

"It's not your fault, Nicky," his Aunt Honoria had said at breakfast just this morning for what must've been the hundredth, perhaps even the thousandth, time. "I do wish you'd stop punishing yourself, dear."

"I'm his father," he'd replied.

"Yes, dear. That you are. But you're not God. Must I keep reminding you of that?"

Nobody needed to remind Doctor Dominic Chiara that he wasn't God. The point had been driven home almost five years ago when his beautiful young wife died, when there had been nothing he could say or do to save her.

He could have saved her, if only she'd given him a chance. He didn't have a doubt in the world about that. But she'd kept her condition secret in order not to jeopardize the child she was carrying. And, even in his grief, he had yet to forgive her for her lies.

Rumor had it that he'd gone back to work with a vengeance after Lara's funeral because being with their son was too painful a reminder of his loss, because he couldn't handle the anger he felt toward the baby who was responsible for his wife's death, because he needed to drown his grief and his guilt in work.

It wasn't true.

He loved his son with all his heart. Rather than a grim reminder, Nick found solace in the boy's resemblance to his mother. The way Leo tilted his head to the left when he was curious. The way his mouth flattened to a thin line when he was thoughtful or anxious. The color of his eyes. The cadence of his laughter. The silky texture of his dark hair. Just like Lara's. Little Leo was his shining star.

He had immersed himself in his work in the hope of ending his feelings of powerlessness, in an attempt to regain some notion of control in his life. If he hadn't spent enough time with the boy in the past few years, it wasn't out of guilt or anger. It was out of fear that he couldn't be a good father until he found his own footing.

Maybe he had. Maybe not. Nick wasn't sure. But it was clear to him now, in light of his son's sudden and strange silence, that his own attempts at healing were self-indulgent. Ready or not, it was time to act like a father, even if he failed.

"There you are, Dr. Chiara." Paula's voice sounded behind him. "I've been looking everywhere for you. You didn't answer your page."

"I didn't hear it," he lied.

He'd heard it, all right. Loud and clear. He'd simply ignored it. No emergency right now was as crucial as the one in his own home. He'd cancelled all his appointments and elective surgeries for the coming month. Doctor Max Schiel had agreed and was more than competent to oversee the health of the royal family for a few weeks. He'd sent the king a copy of his letter to the hospital chief of staff. Because the king was familiar with and was quite sympathetic to the situation with Leo, Nick wasn't anticipating any royal objections.

"I'm on leave, Paula. Starting now."

He looked at his watch. It was already later than he'd expected to remain at the hospital. "The staff is supposed to forward all my calls and refer all my patients to Doctor Schiel until further notice."

"I know that," Paula said, a bit testily. She had, after all, typed his letter for him this morning. She had even congratulated him on his decision before hand-delivering the letter to the chief of staff as well as to the palace. "It wasn't a professional call. It was from your Aunt Honoria. Apparently Leo flushed one of his toys this morning and the plumbing is backed up. Your aunt seemed rather flummoxed by it all, and wanted to know if there was a particular plumber whom she ought to call."

Nick laughed out loud, something he hadn't done in a long time, startling himself as well as his secretary.

"What's so funny about a backed-up toilet?" she asked.

"Nothing, actually," he answered, still chuckling as he removed his stethoscope and shrugged out of his lab coat. "It just sounds—I don't know—so damned normal."

"Well… Yes. I suppose it is. If you like that sort of normalcy." Paula took his lab coat from him and proceeded to fold it. "I hope everything goes well for you and little Leo, Doctor Chiara," she said with soft sincerity.

"Thank you, Paula."

"Will the two of you be going on holiday?"

"Perhaps. I'm not sure yet. But I am sure that whatever we do, it will be just the two of us. No cooks. No housekeepers. No nannies. I'm giving them all the boot this afternoon. I intend to send my aunt away on a long-deserved vacation, as well. For the next four weeks, it's just Leo and me."

"That will be nice," she said.

"Yes." Nick smiled, something else he didn't do much anymore. "It will be very nice."

After Sarah's unexpectedly pleasant audience with the king, Sophia Strezzi returned in all her chilly splendor to accompany Sarah across the palace grounds to the residence of Sir Dominic Chiara and his son. It hardly seemed possible, but the appointment secretary was even less friendly than she had been earlier.

There wasn't time for a tour of the palace, she claimed, hustling Sarah out a side door. "Some other time perhaps."

Moments later, when Sarah commented on the beauty and charm of the landscaping, Sophia merely sniffed in response. Sarah's admiration of the sculptures and fountains that were scattered across the grounds was met with yet another disdainful sniff. When she commented on the lovely climate and the gentle breeze, the woman gave a distinct and dismissive snort.

Fine. Okay. Forget the small talk and all the silly chitchat. Sarah wasn't some goggle-eyed tourist, for heaven's sake. She was a professional, here in Montebello to do a job for Signorina Strezzi's boss. The freaking king!

She was about to announce just that when they passed a small stucco residence that showed signs of a recent fire. One window was boarded up on a badly scorched wall. Broken terra cotta tiles from the roof littered a portion of the yard. Pieces of yellow police tape still fluttered from doorknobs and one or two tree trunks. "When did this happen?" she asked.

Sophia stopped on the cobbled walkway and stared rather glumly at the house. "About three weeks ago."

Sarah blinked. Three weeks? That was presumably the same time the little boy stopped speaking. She wondered… No. It was just too obvious. Far too easy. Any untrained layman, even an idiot could make the logical connection between the fire and a trauma-induced silence. Surely they had already ruled this out.

"How close is the Chiara residence?" she asked.

"Just down the walk." Sophia pivoted away from the burnt house and resumed walking.

After gazing at the place a moment longer, Sarah

jogged to catch up. "You don't happen to know if Doctor Chiara's son witnessed the fire, do you?"

"I have no idea."

Not one she was willing to share, anyway. Sarah made a mental note to inquire about where young Leo Chiara had been when the fire took place. Odd that the king hadn't mentioned it as a possible source of the boy's silence, but at this point she could only assume that the incident had been rejected as a possible cause. Still, she needed to rule it out for herself.

The walkway angled to the left, around a huge oleander bush in magnificent bloom, and Sarah saw a small house not so different from the damaged one behind her.

"Here we are," Sophia announced. "This is the guest cottage where Sir Dominic and his son reside."

Cottage. Good grief. That was a bit like calling the palace a mere house. The place before her looked large enough to be a rambling three- or four-bedroom house. Its yard, an extension of the palace grounds, was clipped and beautifully landscaped. The only giveaway that it was home to a child was a bright blue-and-yellow plastic trike near the front door.

She followed Sophia to the door. The appointment secretary didn't reach for the doorbell immediately, but rather lifted a hand to her head, searching for stray wisps of hair. After that, she subtly adjusted the lapels and seams of her navy suit coat while she drew in a deep breath. They were the actions of a woman who wanted to look somewhat more than merely presentable. They were the gestures, the tiny unconscious tics, of a woman who wanted to look really, really good for someone special.

So that was it! The icy Sophia was in heat! Her coolness and apparent disdain had nothing to do with Sarah, per se. She was merely being territorial, reacting to the presence of another female on a turf she considered exclusively her own. It made perfect sense, now that Sarah thought about it. Sir Dominic was a widower, an undoubtedly mature and wealthy widower, so naturally the man must be considered quite a catch.

She was briefly tempted to reassure Sophia that she was already spoken for and had no interest in the old coot other than helping his son, but then she decided, rather than being so kind and forthcoming, she'd let this female Popsicle shiver in her black pumps a while. It served her right.

They waited several awkward moments, side by side, before the door was opened by an elderly woman whose bright purple silk, tent-size caftan filled the entire doorway. The woman was enormous, nearly the size of the Statue of Liberty, and just as regal, and obviously disappointed to discover who had rung her bell. The smile she wore immediately disappeared.

"Oh, dear. Oh, drat. I was so in hopes it would be the plumber," she said, taking the two women in from head to toe. "I don't suppose you are, are you? Plumbers? No. You couldn't be, I'm sure. What a pity."

Sleek Sophia seemed a bit taken aback. She blinked her big chocolate eyes. "Good afternoon, Lady Satherwaite. Let me introduce myself. I'm Sophia Strezzi, appointment secretary to the Sebastianis. At His Majesty's request, I've brought..."

"Oh, dear. Oh, drat. I do wish you were a plumber." The big woman's ring-laden fingers plucked at the neckline of her caftan. "Leo flushed his Mr. Potato Head this morning and we're all stopped up."

Sarah burst out laughing. She hadn't the vaguest idea who this queen-size, tent-garbed woman was, but she already liked her tremendously. It was the first moment since her arrival in this Mediterranean monarchy that she felt a kind of normalcy, as if Montebello wasn't just some fairy-tale place, but very real and connected to the world with all its fun toys and humdrum difficulties, including stopped-up toilets.

At the sound of Sarah's laughter, huge Lady Satherwaite laughed, too. A booming, joyful sound. She gazed at Sarah, her eyes twinkling beneath her great, gray eyebrows. "I don't know who you are, young lady, but I do like the sound of you."

But standing beside her, Sophia did not seem amused. Not in the least. In fact, Sarah could've sworn she heard the royal appointment secretary growl deep in her throat.

"Is Sir Dominic on the premises?" Sophia asked, adjusting her glasses and launching herself on tiptoe to peer over the purple mountain majesty of the woman's wide shoulders.

"No, he's not, damn the luck. I've had him paged at the hospital, but there's been no response as yet. You don't happen to know if the palace employs a plumber, do you, dear? One would think so considering all the commodes they must have over there." She angled her head in the direction from which Sarah had just come.

"I'm afraid I'm not familiar with any of the maintenance personnel," Sophia told her. She was obviously a woman who disliked discussing plumbing of any sort, even royal. "Do you expect Sir Dominic soon, madam?"

Lady Satherwaite's gaze, no longer twinkling but rather clouded with suspicion, shifted to Sophia. "Who did you say you were, dear?"

"I'm the royal appointments secretary, and I've brought Ms. Sarah Hunter, the new..."

"The new nanny! Well, why didn't you say so?" The big woman reached for Sarah's hands, grasping them in her own. "Come in. Come in. I can't tell you how happy I am that you've arrived."

Before she knew what was happening, Sarah found

herself being yanked across the threshold, while Sophia was left sputtering behind her.

"Lady Satherwaite, one moment, please," the secretary protested. "The king has expressly requested that I speak with you regarding Ms. Hunter's duties, and if possible, I'd very much like to confer with Sir Dominic."

"Oh, bother." The woman lifted her several chins with a resounding snort, which made her appear like a grizzly bear in a purple gown. "She's a nanny in disguise. What more do you need to tell me? Marcus and I have already spoken about this, and at some length, I might add. I suppose he led you to believe that this was his idea."

"Well, His Majesty did say that—"

"Yes, yes. I'm sure he did," the woman said dismissively.

The royal appointments secretary wasn't ready to be dismissed, however. "Perhaps if I spoke with Sir Dominic…"

"By all means, dear. Do give Nicky a call. And if you'd inquire at the palace about a plumber, I'd be most grateful." Lady Satherwaite shoved Sarah out of the way of the door, which she proceeded to slam in Sophia Strezzi's face.

Then the purple giant sighed as she smiled down at a rather bewildered Sarah. "Tea, dear? I'm so happy you've arrived to help our precious little Leo."

* * *

Precious little Leo, as Sarah soon discovered, had been banished to his room and was in solitary confinement, decreed by his great aunt, following the Mr. Potato Head incident. When she followed Lady Satherwaite to the nursery, they found the little boy sound asleep, surrounded by stuffed animals and with his thumb happily nestled in his mouth.

"The little imp," his great aunt whispered. "We're worried sick about this not speaking business, but that doesn't mean we've given him carte blanche in the behavior department. Silent or not, the child knows there are certain unavoidable consequences.

"I believe you professionals refer to it as time out," Lady Satherwaite said a few moments later with a somewhat dismissive sniff while she sipped her tea in the shade of an umbrella on the little terrace behind the guest cottage.

"Well, it is a more neutral expression," Sarah replied. "It doesn't sound quite so punitive."

"Punitive, schmunitive." The big woman shook her head and rattled the many bracelets that decorated both her wrists. "Confining Leo and his imagination to the nursery is far from a punishment, my dear. Believe me. That child can amuse himself for hours on end with nothing more than a paper clip and a rubber band."

"He has an active imagination, then?"

"Oh, my, yes! I'm sure it comes from his father's side of the family. His mother's people are quite dreary."

After half an hour over tea and iced ginger snaps, Sarah had learned far more about Lady Satherwaite than she had about little Leo. Her first impression— that she liked the older lady tremendously—still held. The woman was somehow larger than life. *Much* larger. And she was quite fascinating. Honoria Satherwaite, a sort of gypsy by her own admission, all three hundred pounds of her, had come to Montebello "decades ago, eons back, practically in the Stone Age," she claimed, with her younger sister, Elspeth.

"We were the original hippies back in those days," Lady Satherwaite said, "although we preferred to think of ourselves as adventuresses or *artistes.* We lived on the beach for a while. Went barefoot. Swam in the moonlight wearing only our smiles. I was, of course, much smaller then." She laughed good-naturedly as she rearranged yards of purple silk around her enormous girth. "And much younger. We slept in hammocks that we wove ourselves. Drank champagne for breakfast. It was quite a time."

"It sounds wonderful," Sarah said in all sincerity. She could live like that for a week or two, she decided, but no longer. Without her work, she'd be restless and quite irritable.

"It was wonderful. Oh, yes, indeed. My late husband, George Satherwaite—the poet? Perhaps you've heard of him?"

Sarah shook her head. "No, I'm sorry. I haven't."

"Oh, well. Doesn't matter. He wasn't a very good poet, anyway. Still, he was the dearest of men. George and I were married right down there in the surf by a Yogi. A lovely ceremony even if I didn't understand a word of it. Over the years I've often wondered if it was completely legal, our union. I suppose it doesn't matter now."

The woman sighed as she continued. "At any rate, one way or another, we managed to have a grand time for ourselves and to thoroughly scandalize most of our relatives back in Merry Olde England. Particularly when my sister, Elspeth, was impregnated by that pirate, Chiara."

"Pirate?" Sarah felt herself slipping back into the fairy-tale kingdom of Montebello again. Kings and queens and knights and palaces. Why not pirates, after all? Why not dragons and court jesters while they were at it?

"Pirate. Gunrunner. Mercenary. Whatever. He performed, how shall I say, undercover work for the king in those days." Her big purple shoulders lifted in a shrug and she jangled her bracelets again. "Pure reprobate, I must say, including the single gold earring and the obligatory black eye patch. He was a sight. Oh, my. Luca was a handsome devil. Nicky looks just like him, as a matter of fact. Even more so now that he's older. Fortunately, he's a bit more civilized than his father.''

"Nicky would be Sir Dominic?" Sarah conjured up an image of a crochety, bandy-legged, one-eyed pirate in a striped shirt and silly black boots. If his aunt was this dramatic, Dominic Chiara probably came across like a mustache-twirling villain in a silent film.

"Yes, of course, dear. Nicky would indeed be Sir Dominic. More tea?''

Sarah immediately held up her hand to block the oncoming teapot. Any more Earl Grey and she'd burst. "I wonder if you'd point the way to a rest room, Lady Satherwaite."

"Through the kitchen, and down the hallway to your right. I'm sure that one is safe from submerged toys. One can only hope. Would you like me to show you the way?''

"No, thanks. I'm sure I can find it.''

"All right then. Have a look out the front for the plumber while you're inside, will you, dear?''

A moment later, after passing through the kitchen, Sarah couldn't remember whether she was supposed to turn right or left. It was a wonder she could even remember why she was here, the way Lady Chatterbox babbled on and on. Not that the woman wasn't fascinating. But still.

She turned left. At least she thought so. Her jet

lag suddenly seemed to be advancing to a critical stage, the one where the only directions she understood were the ones to a bed. After she passed along a short corridor and through a comfortable living room, she angled around a large sofa into another corridor and chose the most likely door for the bathroom.

Well, she was half right. It was indeed a bathroom, but the blue giraffes and yellow elephants on the wallpaper were a pretty good clue that this was young Leo's domain rather than a rest room reserved for guests. The second and perhaps most convincing clue that it was a child's bathroom was the man who was kneeling beside the commode and just that moment producing one dripping but still smiling Mr. Potato Head from its depths.

"You must be the plumber."

It was a totally lame thing to say, she thought. Of course he was the plumber, even though he didn't look like any plumber she had ever seen. Those guys tended toward beer guts and visible butt cleavage. This guy...

This guy was...well...much as she hated the expression, "hunk" was the first word that popped into her head, and just about the only word that described the man before her. Other than perfection.

His eyes were a sensuous, almost delicious brown, somewhere between a Hershey's kiss and a Kraft caramel. He was clean shaven, but there was still the suggestion of dark beard along his strong jawline. His nose was slightly aquiline, perfectly carved but for the tiny jog to the right that signified a brief encounter with a fist or some immovable object in his past. His hair was dark, neatly clipped and just beginning to silver at the temples.

He was a Greek god in faded jeans and a pale blue Oxford cloth shirt, its sleeves rolled up to expose tan, perfectly muscled forearms. He reminded her of What's His Name on that TV show. That was a pretty good clue that this was some sort of jet-lag-induced fantasy.

Oh, God. Was she drooling? Sarah wondered all of a sudden.

"You must be the plumber," she said again, sounding even more lame than she had the first time, because the guy probably didn't speak English anyway.

But, miracle of miracles, he did.

"So it would seem," he said in a voice just hinting of an Italian accent. Which meant he was a Roman god, of course, not a Greek one.

Then he stood. To anyone else he might have seemed like a plumber getting to his feet in the cramped space of a bathroom, but to Sarah—thoroughly succumbing now to the ravages of altered time zones—he seemed more like Apollo rising from the white tiled floor until he reached a perfect six foot, two inches. She could hardly breathe, which struck her as odd because there was plenty of room in her chest now that her heart had plunged to the pit of her stomach.

Then he smiled. Sarah almost fainted.

"Who are you?" he asked.

Um…

Good question.

"The ninny," she said.

Oh, God.

"No, I mean the nanny. I'm the new nanny." She reached out and grabbed the wet toy from his hand. "Thank you so much for rescuing Mr. Potato Head."

Then she turned and fled, praying it was in the right direction.

Chapter 3

Nick found his aunt on the terrace, afternoon sunlight glinting off her many rings and bracelets, her great purple garment billowing in the soft breeze.

Honoria Satherwaite was far more than an aunt. She was the closest thing to a mother to him, having raised him single-handedly since he was six, after his parents, still unmarried at the time, had sailed off for Crete one April afternoon and never returned. It was only years later that Nick learned he, too, would have been lost at sea if Honoria hadn't snatched him off the yacht, railing at her sister that ''the boy will be a bloody idiot if you keep taking him out of school for months on end.''

He didn't recall that particular incident, and he

didn't remember ever missing his parents. When it came to memories of his youth, mostly he recalled feeling safe and secure and very much adored by the big woman who made him the center of her universe.

Unorthodox as she was, his aunt had done everything in her power to raise him not only properly, but also quite traditionally.

She might have dressed like a gypsy herself, but she sent her nephew to the Boys' Academy in San Sebastian every day in the strict uniform of blue blazer and red tie. Despite her own bizarre or nonexistent religious beliefs, she insisted he attend Sunday school and services each week at the basilica of San Felipe, where he became a model altar boy. And even though the woman didn't know a soccer ball from a tennis ball, she sat through every game or match he ever had.

During his teenage years, whenever he indicated an interest in a career—whether it was being a musician, a race car driver, or a professional deep sea diver—she'd always supported him wholeheartedly by saying, "That would be lovely, Nicky dear, *after* you've gone to medical school."

She was lavish with praise, slow to anger, quick to envelop him in hugs and shower him with kisses. Where young Nick Chiara was concerned, Honoria Satherwaite's heart was as large as the rest of her, if not several sizes larger.

Although he'd succeeded in getting her to give up

her precious cigarettes, he'd stopped badgering her about her diet years ago. The woman was close to eighty now and still healthy as a draft horse. She'd probably outlive him. Whatever success he'd achieved in his life was because of her. No question about it.

There was probably only a single time he hadn't taken his aunt's advice. That was when he'd asked her what she thought of Lara Davis-Finch, the girl he wanted to marry.

"She's lovely," Aunt Honoria had said. "She's the sort of woman who will always tell her husband exactly what he wants to hear, dear."

At the time, those words had sounded more like praise than a caution to Nick. Now, of course, he knew it meant that Lara would hide any truth that she considered ugly from him, would lie about her health rather than distress him for a single moment, would tell him everything was wonderful when it wasn't. After Lara died and left him with six-month-old Leo, it was his Aunt Honoria who had once again come to his rescue.

He wondered now if that had been a mistake. With Honoria to depend on, he'd been able to bury himself in his work without worrying for a single moment about Leo's well-being. With Honoria in charge, he'd been able to convince himself that all was well on the domestic front. She'd made it so easy for him.

Still, mistake or not, it wasn't too late to make

some changes. Nick strode out onto the terrace, prepared to do just that.

Upon seeing him, his aunt waved a ring-laden
hand while her bracelets clacked and jingled on her
meaty arm. "There you are, Nicky. Tea, dear?"

"No, thanks." He bent to kiss her cheek.

"Are you sure? It's oolong. Your favorite."

"I'm sure," he said, settling in the chair across
the table from her, narrowing his gaze, girding himself for battle. "There's a new nanny, I see. Honoria,
I thought we agreed…"

"Oh, did you meet her, darling? Poor thing came
racing out here a few moments ago with her eyes
practically pinwheeling, babbling something about a
plumber and twisted time zones and raging jet lag. I
immediately sent her off for a nap." She reached for
a scone, popped it into her mouth, indicating that, as
far as she was concerned, the discussion was over.

Not by a long shot.

"No more nannies. At least not for a while. We
discussed this at length, Honoria, when we let the
last one go. I assumed we were in agreement that it
was best for Leo. As soon as the woman wakes up
from her nap, I'm going to give her the sack."

"I'm afraid you can't, dear," she said coolly.

Nick raised an eyebrow, knowing he didn't need
to ask her to elaborate.

"I hired her, you see." She reached for another

scone. ''The young lady works for me, and I haven't the slightest intention of firing her.''

''Honoria…'' he grumbled.

''The subject is closed to discussion,'' she said. ''Try one of these scones, dear. They're quite good.''

Nick ripped his fingers through his hair out of sheer frustration. Much as he loved her, the woman could be as irritating and infuriating as…

''Don't be cross, Nicky. It's not good for the digestion, and it makes your eyebrows knot and your handsome face look frightfully demonic. Besides, if it's any consolation, Ms. Hunter hasn't signed on with us permanently. She's only here for two or three weeks on a trial basis.''

She reached for the teapot, and while refilling her cup, she said, ''She's lovely, don't you think?''

''Who?''

''The nanny, of course. Ms. Hunter.''

Was she lovely? Yes, Nick supposed she was, now that he thought about it. He really didn't notice women much these days, not in any physical sense anyway. He'd only seen her for a moment, and a rather befuddled one at that, during which she apparently had believed he was a plumber. He conjured up a quick vision of her pretty face with its startled green eyes and generous mouth.

''Does Leo like her?'' he asked. ''That's really all that matters.''

''He hasn't met her yet. She only arrived an hour

or so ago, and Leo was sound asleep. I don't know why he wouldn't like her, though. She's absolutely charming.''

"He doesn't need to be charmed, Honoria. He needs to speak, for God's sake. I was hoping, if the two of us could be alone for the next few weeks, that he might come around.''

"He will, Nicky. I know that in my heart.''

She reached out to pat his hand just as the telephone on the table began to ring. His aunt glared at the small black object next to the teapot and muttered, "Now who do you suppose that could be? I don't know why I ever let you talk me into one of these infernal machines. They're so bloody intrusive. You answer it, darling, will you? Tell whomever it is that I'm otherwise occupied.''

He'd insisted on the continual presence of the cell phone in case his elderly aunt had any unexpected problems with her health. Much as she claimed to detest the thing, she'd apparently given the number out to several dozen of her friends.

As soon as Nick said hello, he regretted it. The caller was a flunky from the palace, intending to remind Lady Satherwaite to remind her nephew that the king was expecting him at the palace this evening to attend a party in honor of Montebello's Olympic committee. Since he was the little country's sole medal winner—a bronze two decades earlier in archery—King Marcus was forever dragging him out on these occasions.

"Yes. All right. I'll be there," he snarled into the phone, then swore after he broke the connection.

"Bad news, dear?"

"I thought I'd cleared all the decks for the next month, but I forgot about the gala for the Olympic committee this evening."

"You'll need a date," she said. "Marcus doesn't like it when there are too many bachelors oozing around at these affairs. It plays havoc with the queen's seating arrangements."

"Well, then, I'll take my favorite girl," he said, winking at her across the table. "Do you feel up to it?"

Before answering, Honoria gazed at him for a long moment. There was a certain wistfulness in her expression, a touch of sadness he rarely saw in his aunt, an emotion he was unable to fathom. He could usually read her so well, but not this time.

"Yes, I most certainly do feel up to it," she said, "but I'd rather poke a sharp stick in my eye than have to sit across a dinner table from Humberto Franchi. That dreadful man is still the grand poobah of the Olympic thing, isn't he?"

Nick nodded.

"Well, then. Thank you, darling, but no thank you. I have a much better idea. Why don't I stay home with Leo, and you escort Ms. Hunter to the gala?"

"Ms. Hunter?"

"The nanny, you ninny."

He shook his head. "I don't think that's a good idea. I'm sure she doesn't—"

Just then, the pager clipped to his belt began to shrill. Damn. He'd forgotten to take it off. The number indicated an emergency call from the hospital. Despite being officially on leave, his conscience wouldn't permit him to ignore it.

"May I use your phone, love?" he asked his aunt.

"By all means, dear."

Honoria Satherwaite ate another scone as she listened to her nephew's conversation on the cell phone. Poor Nicky. He was far too conscientious to ignore a call from the hospital. She liked to think that she was at least partly responsible for his dedication to his profession and somewhat responsible for the fine man he had become.

God only knows how he might have turned out if he'd been raised by her foolish sister and that pirate. God only knows how her own life would have turned out if she hadn't marched little Nicky off their boat that April day three decades ago. The hand of God. Fate. Kismet. Whatever had impelled her to grab the child and take him home, it was the most fortunate thing Honoria had ever done.

She'd done her best to raise him to be a strong, responsible man. She'd tried hard not to bully him into making the right decisions, but rather to gently guide him. All in all, she hadn't done a bad job.

Except for his marriage to Lara. Nicky never could see that they were terribly ill-suited to one another, and he would have fallen on a sword before admitting he'd made a mistake in marrying the girl. But even that dark cloud turned out to have its own silver lining because of little Leo.

She looked across the table now and watched Nick scowl as he spoke into the phone. It had been so long since her nephew had laughed, she almost couldn't recall the sound of it.

"I need to return to the hospital," he said when he put the telephone down. "One of my patients is in trouble."

"Oh, dear."

"Sorry, love." He rose, walked around the table, and kissed the top of her head. "I'll take my formal clothes with me, then shower and change at the hospital. I won't be home late. Are you sure you don't want to come with me? I could send a car for you."

"I think not, dear. Give my regards to the king and queen."

She watched him nearly sprint across the terrace, full of purpose, anxious to assist his patient. How he thought he was going to be happy taking a month away from work was a mystery to Honoria.

And she so wanted him to be happy.

Suddenly, just as her intuition had told her that

Lara was the wrong woman to make him happy, Honoria felt a little *ping* of intuition now. It struck her as so obvious, she wondered why she hadn't thought of it before.

The right woman had just arrived.

Chapter 4

Sarah stepped out of the shower, shaking her wet head and reaching blindly for a towel. This couldn't be happening to her, could it? How in the world had she allowed herself to get roped into going to a party? And not roped into just any party...nooo...but a big deal, fancy schmancy, annual bash at the palace? And worse—on a night like tonight when her jet-lagged brain was still back in San Francisco while her body was functioning like a zombie in Montebello?

A while ago, when Lady Satherwaite had awakened her by tapping her shoulder—gently at first and then rather insistently—Sarah hadn't even been certain where she was. She'd been dreaming about War-

ren and something about balancing checkbooks and
whether or not to cut the crusts off sandwiches, both
subjects having an endless fascination for her fiancé
in the dream while Sarah kept exclaiming "Who
cares, Warren? It's just a dream anyway. None of
this is real, for heaven's sake. I'm not even here.
Neither are you." He could be such a twit, even
when she was asleep.

"I need an enormous favor from you, Sarah,
dear," Lady Satherwaite had said, and then, while
Sarah slowly ratcheted herself awake, the woman had
gone on to explain, quite dramatically, that Sir Dominic was in dire, even drastic need of a companion
for some big deal at the palace. Old Sir Dominic
needed a date! Good grief.

"I can't," Sarah answered automatically and
pretty firmly for somebody still half asleep.

"Of course you can."

After that, every excuse she dredged up from her
soggy brain was immediately put down. The woman
wouldn't take no for an answer.

"I don't want to go," she told her.

"Nonsense," Lady Satherwaite replied.

Sarah's best and final argument—that she didn't
have a thing to wear for such an occasion—had
failed miserably when Honoria Satherwaite smiled
triumphantly and said, "Not to worry, dear. I've already seen to that."

And so she had. After wrapping a big, fluffy towel

around herself and scampering back to her room, Sarah discovered the most beautiful dress she'd ever seen in her life waiting for her, spread out upon her bed. It was a deep, rich, red satin, the color of geraniums, with a long, graceful bell of a skirt and a simple strapless bodice. Stunningly simple. Exquisitely elegant. The sort of dress that Audrey Hepburn might have worn in a film with Cary Grant.

"I think these shoes will do," Lady Satherwaite said, fluttering into the bedroom, a pair of delicate strappy silver sandals dangling from her hand. "Do you like the gown?"

"It's gorgeous."

"I haven't a doubt in the world that it will fit. You look to be about the same size as Lara." Her gaze dropped a few inches. "A bit bustier, however, I must say."

"Lara?"

"Nicky's late wife. I thought you knew."

Sarah made a tiny gasping sound. "Oh, I can't wear her dress, then. What would Sir Dominic think? Surely just the sight of it would bring back painful memories."

"Actually, Nicky's never seen this gown. Lara bought it and hid it in the back of her closet to inspire herself to get her figure back after their baby was born." She sighed. "Alas, that wasn't to be. Poor girl. But as far as my nephew is concerned, there are no memories attached to it at all. It's just a frock he's never seen. I don't think he even notices such things, to tell you the truth.''

''Well, then I suppose it's all right.'' Sarah reached out to touch the elegant satin of the skirt. It was probably a designer original. It probably cost more than she made in six months at the clinic. It would be sort of fun, actually, wearing it for one night. She'd feel a bit like Cinderella.

''It really is gorgeous,'' she said with a sigh. ''But I—''

''Of course it is. No arguing now, Sarah. There simply isn't time. Give a shout when you've got it on, my dear, and I'll come help with the zipper in back.''

Just moments later, Sarah had barely gotten herself into the dress when Lady Satherwaite floated back into the room like some huge, purple fairy godmother.

''Oh, my dear! Don't you look divine?'' she exclaimed. ''Just look.'' She whirled Sarah around to face the full-length mirror on the closet door, then tugged up the zipper.

Well, she didn't look horrible, she thought. In fact, she looked far better than she felt on just a few hours sleep. Her eyes weren't bloodshot or half mast or anything. Her complexion wasn't gray. She looked not horrible. In fact, she looked okay. For a zombie, anyway. As for the dress, it was absolutely amazing. It looked as if it belonged on the cover of *Vogue*.

"Brush your hair a bit, dear," Lady Satherwaite said, "and put on just a skimming of lipstick. I'll call a car for you."

"I'd really rather walk," Sarah said. "The palace is just around the corner."

"Nonsense."

Just then a small face with large brown eyes appeared in the doorway. Large and very curious brown eyes beneath a mop of soft brown hair. Sarah felt her heart melt at the sight of the little boy.

Children, almost all of them, had the most endearing eyes. The scientist in her was aware that this was simply because of proportion, that children's eyes were still quite large in comparison to their little faces. But, scientist or not, deep in her heart she still believed it was because their souls shone through more readily, more clearly than any adult's.

"Hello," she said. "You must be Leo." She knelt on the floor in a huge billow of red satin, and held out both her hands. "I'm Sarah. And I've been waiting to meet you."

The child aimed a quizzical glance at Lady Satherwaite.

"You may come in, my dearest," she said. "Come on, then. It's quite all right, Leo. Shake hands with your new nanny. There's a good little gentleman."

As he walked from the doorway in his blue Winnie the Pooh footed jammies, Sarah attempted to study his expression without appearing too clinical, or even too interested. He didn't seem to be the least bit fearful, or even particularly shy. The boy made direct eye contact with her. In fact, his gaze never wavered from her face as he approached. It was almost as if he was trying to identify her. Studying her face as if she was standing in a lineup.

His small hands were warm when he reached out to place them in hers. Trust shone in his big brown eyes. A tiny smile flirted at the corners of his mouth.

"Oh, do be careful, Leo darling," his great aunt moaned somewhere above them. "You're trampling her dress."

"That's all right." Sarah kept a sure, but gentle grip on his hands while her eyes stayed fixed on his. "I don't mind at all. I'm just so happy to finally meet you, Leo."

His smile didn't evaporate, as she might have expected with a troubled child. If anything, it seemed to increase a little bit. Sarah took that as an excellent sign.

"We're going to have so much fun together, Leo. I can tell that already," she told him. "I've brought lots of toys for us to play with. I hope we can get started tomorrow after we eat breakfast."

She made it a point not to ask him a direct question because she didn't want the boy to feel threatened by her in any way or the least bit pressured to speak. But he would. In his own good time. With her help. And soon, perhaps. She was certain of it. Now, even more than before, she wished she didn't have to attend this wretched affair at the palace just because old Sir Dominic didn't have a date.

"Run along to bed now, young man," Lady Satherwaite said. "I'll be in for your prayers in just a few minutes."

"Good night, Leo," Sarah said softly. She reached up to ruffle his hair. "See you tomorrow. We're going to have so much fun. I can't wait."

The feet of his pj's made little brushing noises on the carpet as he turned and skipped out of the room.

"That went rather well," Lady Satherwaite said with a pronounced sigh. She sounded almost relieved, as if she hadn't expected their first encounter to go well at all.

Sarah got to her feet carefully inside the voluminous yards of red satin. "Yes, I think it did. He's adorable."

"Quite adorable," she said with obvious pride. "And quite intelligent, too."

"You mentioned his prayers, Lady Satherwaite. Leo doesn't actually say them out loud, does he?" she asked, hoping against hope that he did. Some children with mutism still chose to verbalize in selected settings or with selected people. If this were the case with Leo, her work would be even easier.

"From your lips to the Almighty's ears," the woman said, rolling her eyes heavenward. "The child hasn't made a peep for nearly three weeks. Not to anyone, as far as I'm aware. Certainly not to his father nor to me. Not even his sweet prayers.''

"Well, I hope it won't be long before he's saying his prayers out loud again," Sarah said, trying not to sound overly optimistic before she had actually begun to work with the child. "I'm anxious to begin working with him tomorrow. What time does Leo usually get up for his breakfast?"

"Seven or seven-thirty. Thereabouts."

"Good. I'll set my alarm for six-thirty so I'll be ready to join him for breakfast."

Lady Satherwaite frowned. "So early, dear? Are you sure you'll be up to it?"

"Yes, of course. Why wouldn't I be?"

"Well, it's bound to be a late night at the palace. No one ever leaves before the king and queen, and they rarely give up the proverbial ghost until well after midnight. Quite the revelers, those two."

"Oh." She didn't mean to sound so disappointed, even though she was. The prospect of being Sir Dominic's date for more than an hour or two was thoroughly depressing.

"You'll have a lovely time, I'm sure. Nicky can be very charming when he puts his mind to it, and he's quite a good dancer."

"That's nice."

Sarah peered into the mirror and ran a trace of lipstick across her mouth. Then she finger-combed her damp hair into a halfway decent style. She didn't want to look too good, actually. The worse she looked, the less the old geezer would be attracted to her. Or so she hoped. Which suddenly reminded her that she didn't have a clue what her date for the evening looked like.

"How will I recognize Sir Dominic?" she asked.

"How…? Oh, my goodness. Well, let me think. Other than being the handsomest man in the room…"

I'll just bet, Sarah thought as she waited for Lady Satherwaite to continue with words like bald, pot-bellied, liver-spotted, and knock-kneed. Jeez. He probably didn't even have his own teeth, and his breath probably reeked of cigars and brandy.

"I know how you'll recognize him," the big woman said. "Nicky will be the only one there this evening wearing an Olympic medal. That should make him quite easy to identify."

"That should work," Sarah said with a last glance in the mirror. "Well, that's the best I can do. Cinderella, as they say, is ready for the ball."

Lady Satherwaite smiled as she gazed at Sarah approvingly, then said, "Oh, how I wish I could change a pumpkin into a coach for you. Do let me call you a car, dear."

Sarah shook her head. "I'm looking forward to the walk," she said. "The fresh air will do me good."

Maybe even keep her awake, she hoped.

* * *

Nick came down the back staircase at the palace after a quick visit with his old pal, Prince Lucas, in the family quarters. The prince continued to do well after his ordeal of the past year following his plane crash. He was lucky to be alive, actually.

As Nick approached the ballroom where the Olympic gala was to take place, it occurred to him that he'd spent a great deal of his life right here in these regal surroundings.

He and Lucas had been the best of friends from grade school on, so from the age of eight or nine, Nick had practically lived here on the weekends. He and Lucas had made prank phone calls from the palace switchboard, dropped water balloons on visiting dignitaries, gone skinny-dipping in the fountains, started a fire in an upstairs trash basket when they'd experimented with cigarettes, done every silly thing that young boys do, and been royally punished for their misdeeds.

The king and queen had been like a second set of parents to him, in addition to his Aunt Honoria. It was the royal family, in fact, who had paid for his medical education. And after Lara died, it was King Marcus himself who had insisted that Nick and his son move onto the palace grounds where the boy could be looked after better.

He hadn't done such a good job with that, had he?

The royal couple was just as concerned about his

son's silence as if Leo were their very own grand-child. They'd been pressuring him hard to take the boy to a psychologist, but they didn't seem to understand that as a physician, Nick felt compelled to rule out all physical causes of his son's mutism before he could begin to consider psychotherapy of any sort.

And now that all the tests had come back either negative or well within normal ranges, and after he'd consulted with some of the best neurologists and ear, nose and throat men on the continent, Nick was finally prepared to take the next step, although what that would be other than spending the next month one-on-one with his son, he wasn't quite sure. With any luck, merely being together all the time would accomplish some sort of miracle in the speech department. In the meantime, he intended to locate and to read everything ever written on the subject of mutism.

He turned into the corridor that led to the ballroom where tonight's festivities were to take place. If he were incredibly lucky, the king and queen would introduce him early on and he would be able to sneak out the palace's back door well before midnight.

"There you are, Sir Dominic. At last. I've been looking all over for you."

The woman who spoke was standing just outside the ballroom doors. She was lovely in a severe sort of way. Nick was certain he knew her—there were always so many familiar faces floating around at affairs like these—but he couldn't come up with a name.

"I'm Sophia Strezzi, the king's appointment secretary," she said, holding out a hand toward him. "We've spoken frequently. Just last week, as a matter of fact."

Had they? Nick couldn't recall. Still, he took her hand and bent to place his lips on the delicate knuckles. The gallant gesture his Aunt Honoria had insisted upon in his youth had become a habit after all these years.

When she withdrew her hand from his, she reached into a small handbag and produced a medal dangling from a ribbon. "I retrieved this from the Olympic exhibit at the museum, at the king's request," she said.

Nick had to bite down on a grin. His bronze medal had been in the royal museum ever since he'd won the damned thing. "The king doesn't trust me with it," he told the appointment secretary, only half in jest.

"His majesty is enormously proud of your accomplishment," she said. "As are we all. Now, if you'll allow me…"

She was tall enough so that Nick merely had to bend a bit for her to ease the ribbon over his head and around his neck. He always forgot how heavy the medal was. Gazing down at the interlocked

Olympic rings, he found himself also gazing at Ms. Strezzi's fingers as they lingered a bit on his chest.

"It came to my attention," she said, "that you didn't have a dinner partner this evening, Sir Dominic. I've taken the liberty of seating myself beside you. I hope you don't mind."

"Not at all," he replied.

The sad truth was that he not only didn't mind, he was totally indifferent to the woman's overtures. It didn't matter that she was quite stunning or that she smelled like gardenias and was obviously attracted to him. The appointment secretary might as well have been a coatrack for all he was attracted to her.

He wondered again when, or if, his sexual desire would return. It had been absent for four years now, ever since Lara's death. He kept intending to make an appointment with Emmanuel Giardello, the hospital's head of urology, even though he was reasonably certain there was nothing physically wrong. His libido was gone. That was all. Shrivelled. Shattered. Gone with the proverbial wind. And he was indifferent to its retrieval.

"Well, I'll see you at dinner, then," he said, sounding far more eager and charming than he felt, as he stepped back from the secretary's lingering hand and proceeded to make his way into the crowded ballroom.

Sarah could hear the music in the distance. It was Mozart, she thought, and quite lovely. She could even see the glow of the palace in the night sky, but damned if she could get there.

Two wrong turns at the same stupid Cupid fountain had brought her practically back to where she started, not too far from the burned-out guest house. The place that had looked rather forbidding by daylight was positively creepy when lit only by the moon and a few of the gaslights scattered about the palace grounds. The acrid smell of the fire was still lingering in the air.

For a minute she wished Warren were with her. Not that she really missed his company, but he was great with directions. A veritable human compass.

He was always so logical.

When he told her "If you're facing west, then north has to be on your right", Sarah always found herself wanting to really irritate him by replying "Well, not necessarily."

The good thing about Warren was he knew how to get there from here. The bad thing was he had no appreciation of what lay between. If something wasn't on his to-do list, he wouldn't even consider doing it. For Warren, everything was black or white, while Sarah tended to see myriad shades of gray. For Warren, two and two always added up to four, while for Sarah, two and two could sometimes be five or even six, depending on how you looked at it.

Which was undoubtedly why she was lost right now, and why she had chosen to marry someone so unlike herself. Lost was not a good way to be. She'd witnessed that firsthand when her brother, Elliot, lost his beloved wife and daughter to a car accident, and then lost himself to years of pain and grief. There had been nothing she could do to help him. Nothing. That was when she vowed she'd never allow herself to suffer a similar loss. What if she couldn't help herself?

The fact that Elliot had recovered, that he had fallen in love again and remarried, hadn't changed Sarah's mind one bit. She would never marry for love. Ever. She wouldn't risk her heart that way.

It was obvious that no one in her family approved of her choice of mates. Particularly her father. That didn't bother her too much because Sarah knew what she needed, and she knew that Warren Dill would make an excellent husband despite the fact that she wasn't in love with him. Actually that's why he was perfect for her—*because* she wasn't in love with him.

He'd never cause her any of the heart-shattering pain she'd witnessed in her brother. Anyway, there was already so much pain associated with her job as a child psychologist, she didn't need it at home, as well. Warren was perfect for her.

If something happened to Warren... Well, she'd be very sad, distraught, even. But her heart wouldn't break. She'd survive.

That is, if she didn't die of exposure and malnutrition right here before she found her way to the palace.

Sarah sighed, concentrated on the golden glow in the sky above the palace, and made her way toward it.

At the edge of the crowded ballroom, half-hidden behind a potted palm, Nick lifted a flute of champagne from a passing waiter's tray, then stared glumly into the dancing bubbles.

He should probably quit this business of kissing women's hands, he told himself. The gesture was altogether too effective. It held sexual implications that he no longer intended, and sensual promises that he couldn't keep. Before his libido had died, he used to love the startled little gasp that lodged in a woman's throat when his lips brushed the back of her hand. Now that little gasp made him want to run a thousand miles away.

It didn't help a bit that women seemed to find him quite attractive, an allure he'd never understood himself whenever he looked in a mirror at a complexion he deemed too swarthy, eyes a little too intense and dark and a constant shadow on his jawline no matter how close he shaved.

It was the pirate in him, his Aunt Honoria said. *Just like your father, God rest his devious soul.* And his father's renegade looks had served Nick well, he had to admit, in his bachelor days when he and

Prince Lucas were known from London to Cairo as the Derelict Duo.

But now his attraction for women merely served to remind him of his loss of interest in them. There wasn't much he *was* interested in these days, except for his work and his son. Nick looked at his watch. Only a few more hours, and then he could escape.

Tomorrow he and Leo—

A flash of red across the ballroom caught his eye, just as he heard the voices of two women rise above the chatter of the crowd.

"What do you mean, I can't attend?" Sarah wailed. "I just don't understand this."

"Your name does not appear on the guest list," Sophia Strezzi said again, stubbornly, a little louder than before, as if she now considered Sarah deaf as well as stupid.

"Probably not," Sarah told her. "It was a last-minute thing. But I promise you, I really am Sir Dominic Chiara's date. Call his aunt. She'll tell you."

"I don't have time to make calls once a gala has begun," the appointment secretary snapped. She tapped a vellum page, lodged in a rich leather binder and calligraphed with neat columns of names, Sarah's obviously not among them. "Look for yourself, if you'd like, Ms. Hunter. It's out of my hands entirely. Only those on the guest list are permitted

into the ballroom. I'm very sorry, but I'm afraid
you'll have to leave.''

Leave? *Leave?!* Sarah didn't think so. Not after
she'd traipsed all over the royal grounds for the past
forty-five minutes trying to get here. Not after she'd
tripped up the palace steps in her long gown, been
stopped at the royal front door, questioned by several
uniformed guards and subsequently wandered into a
restricted area, setting off a shrill alarm. After that,
she'd been nearly strip-searched only to discover that
there was a magnetic anti-theft device sewn into the
hem of her gown.

She hadn't wanted to come to the stupid party in
the first place, but—by God—now that she was here,
she was damn well going to stay here.

"I'm Sir Dominic Chiara's guest," she said. Date
sounded a bit adolescent, if not provincial in this elegant setting.

"Not according to the official list," the woman
insisted, raising her voice another notch.

Sarah followed suit. "Then call Lady Satherwaite,
will you? She'll explain."

"I really can't do that. Please leave, Ms. Hunter,
or I'll be forced to call the palace security."

Sarah stood her ground, clenching her fists and
gritting her teeth. She remembered how this Strezzi
dame had behaved at Sir Dominic's house earlier,
and it suddenly occurred to her why the woman
didn't want her hanging around. Sophia wanted old

Sir Nicky unaccompanied, unencumbered and all to her snarly, officious little self this evening.

In fact, the woman was gazing over Sarah's shoulder right this minute as if she were searching for her knight in ancient armor among the crowd. The look on Sophia's face was positively luminous with anticipation, just gooey with adoration for the doddering old coot.

"Why don't we just cut to the chase here, cookie," Sarah said, no longer willing to play this female's silly little game. "Let's ask Sir Dominic, shall we? Let's let him decide whether or not I'm his guest tonight."

The oddest smile worked its way across Sophia Strezzi's lips just then—triumphant and very, very sly—a smirk actually-before she purred, "Ask him yourself, Ms. Hunter. He's standing directly behind you."

"Good," Sarah snapped. "Fine."

She whirled around and found herself staring into a bronze medal embossed with five Olympic rings. This was her guy, all right. Good.

She lifted her gaze to his face.

Oh, God.

This really wasn't happening, was it?

It was the jet lag, obviously, and the lack of sleep.

She was hallucinating.

And when the hunky plumber grasped her hand and brought it to his lips, Sarah thought she just might pass out.

Chapter 5

Nick recognized the petite nanny instantly. He had never seen a female face, much less any human face, progress through so many emotions in the space of a few seconds. It was like watching a charming cartoon.

First came the astonishment that slackened her jaw and widened her green eyes. After that came the bewilderment that tugged at her finely shaped eyebrows and twitched at the corners of her mouth. A lovely mouth, Nick couldn't help but notice. It was lush without seeming obvious. Soft and pliable and perfectly shaped. He had to force his gaze back to the rest of her face.

Next came a kind of embarrassment or consternation that heightened the color of her cheeks, and then—finally, outlandishly, and so delightfully—came the amusement that brightened her entire countenance like a sudden ray of sunshine.

The nanny burst out laughing.

"Obviously you're not the plumber," she said when she was finally able to speak.

"Not this evening anyway, Ms. Hunter," Nick said. He remembered he'd idly thought she was somewhat attractive when he'd seen her earlier today. The light in Leo's bathroom must've been bad. The nanny was absolutely lovely. Far more beautiful than any other woman in the room. Perhaps in the entire world.

Far and away more beautiful than the king's appointment secretary, who was wedging herself like a human hatchet between them at the moment.

"Ms. Hunter is not on the royal guest list, Sir Dominic. I've checked and I've rechecked," she said, tapping a long fingernail on her sacred document. "I've been trying quite politely to explain the situation to her, but she doesn't seem to comprehend the problem. I'm sure you, of all people, understand that it's impossible to abandon protocol at the last minute."

The woman's voice was rising with each successive word. The hand that wasn't clutching the list was making harsh chopping movements in the air.

"It simply isn't done," she screeched. "His Majesty would be horribly upset if I were to…"

The nanny's laughter had subsided enough for her to say, "Wait a minute. Wait just a minute, will you? This isn't the end of the world as we know it, Ms. Strezzi. Good grief. It's a party, that's all. A silly dinner dance. Well, I realize it's a royal one, but still…"

"There are rules," the woman snapped. "There is palace protocol, not to mention security." Her dark eyes narrowed on the nanny.

Nick was tempted to put an end to the confrontation between the two females, but his curiosity suddenly got the better of him. He wanted to see how the nanny handled herself under the stress of Sophia Strezzi. Up until now, Ms. Hunter had shown an ingrained politeness and great restraint, he decided, but he detected a growing fire in her green eyes along with a stiffening of her bare shoulders and a stubborn lifting of her chin.

"You're not on my list," the appointments secretary said, this time stabbing a finger close to the nanny's delicate collarbone.

That was enough. Nick was fully prepared to step between them just as the Hunter woman rolled her eyes toward the gilded ceiling and said, "This is ridiculous. I don't even want to be here!"

She whirled around like a small crimson tornado then and took off down the corridor.

Ms. Strezzi uttered a sound that wavered somewhere between a snort and a growl. "Americans," she said, tacking on a dismissive sigh. The word sounded vaguely like *barbarians*. "It never ceases to amaze me that some people show so little regard for manners and tradition. Don't you agree, Sir Dominic?"

"I do agree," he said solemnly, his gaze still locked on the retreating red gown, the fetching sway of the nanny's derriere as she hustled along the corridor, the men who turned to take a second look, and some a third after she'd passed by them. "I wonder if you'd do me a great favor, Ms. Strezzi?"

Nick glanced at her now in time to see the quick but distinct flare of desire in her dark eyes.

"Yes, of course. Why, I'd do anything for you, Sir Dominic," she murmured. "Anything. I...I thought you knew. All you have to do is ask."

"I appreciate that," he replied while he lifted the ribbon and bronze medal and eased them over his head. "It's traditional to have my medal front and center at this annual affair. I wouldn't want to ruin the king's expectations, or the Olympic committee's, for that matter. So, I was wondering..."

He held the ribbon in front of her, high, as if about to encircle her head.

"I was wondering, Ms. Strezzi, if you'd do me the great honor of wearing it for me this evening?"

Nick heard the woman's breath catch in her throat

and actually saw her pulse throb in her neck, and for a fleeting second he felt like the lowest of heels, the rottenest of rogues, the worst of wretches. Ah, well. It wasn't the first time, and it probably wouldn't be the last.

"It would be my pleasure, Sir Dominic," she whispered huskily, then licked her lips as he slowly fit the ribbon over her head and laid the medal against the bodice of her dress.

"There," he said, gazing down at her. "It looks wonderful on you. Just grand. Very traditional."

She glanced down. "Yes. Thank you."

"You're most welcome. And if you'll see that it gets back to the museum tomorrow, I'll be most appreciative. Good night, Ms. Strezzi. Please give my regrets to the king and queen."

He turned just in time to see the hem of the red gown disappear like the flicker of a flame around a corner, just in time to feel his indifferent heart kick in a few extra beats.

He followed as fast as he could.

With each step down the palace stairs, Sarah cursed somebody else. She started with the Strezzi dame, wishing she'd said something a bit more clever, a *lot* more clever than just "I'm leaving." Actually she wished now that she'd told the royal appointments secretary just where she could put her guest list. In fact, Sarah almost wished she'd done it for her.

Then she cursed her father for sending her to this Mediterranean monarchy, this medieval paradise, in the first place. That was just nuts, flying her halfway across the world when there were dozens, probably even hundreds, of available therapists, competent ones, closer to Montebello. There was Renata Falci in Rome, after all, and Dr. George Stern in Geneva, both of them world famous and miracle workers when it came to troubled children. There was Russell Burke in London. There was Hanna Vrooman in the Netherlands. What had her father been thinking? Assuming he was thinking at all.

She cursed King Marcus, too, who presumably had asked her father for advice. She added another little expletive for Lady Satherwaite, who'd been in cahoots with the king.

She tripped again on the hem of her dress, then hissed a few well chosen oaths.

Just for good measure, she cursed her fiancé, Warren Dill. If they'd gotten married when he first asked her, the way Sarah had wanted to, this probably wouldn't be happening to her now. But no…Warren wanted a wedding with all the proper traditions and trimmings. Of course he did. He wouldn't be paying for it. Her parents would.

Last but hardly least, she cursed Sir Dominic Chiara. Roundly. Soundly. Up one side and down the other of his elegant black tuxedo. How dare he turn out to be the gorgeous plumber instead of the old geezer she'd imagined him to be? How dare he have those gooey brown eyes, so dark they were nearly black? Not chocolate like normal brown eyes, but lovely, luscious licorice. How dare he wear a five o'clock shadow so sexily when most men with even a suggestion of stubble on their jaws looked like bums? The son of a pirate, indeed! The bluebeard!

God bless it. How dare the man kiss her hand and send a jolt of pure electricity through her when she had deliberately unplugged herself from those sort of attractions? And he hadn't zapped her just once, but twice—first as a plumber, then as a certified knight. Or a duke or a baron or an earl. Whatever the hell the Sir stood for.

Sir…as in surprised!

As in surreal.

As in he certainly wasn't what she'd expected little Leo's father to be, although why she had assumed Sir Dominic Chiara was a withered and doddering old codger was beyond her recollection right now. Had her father said something to lead her astray? Or was it the king who'd given her the impression that Dr. Chiara was an elderly widower? Was it something Lady Satherwaite had said?

No wonder Sophia Strezzi had behaved like a bitch in heat this afternoon and then again this evening.

Sarah probably would, too, if she felt her territory was threatened by another woman.

Not that she had to worry about jealousy with Warren. That was another reason she was so comfortable with her choice of a mate. If he left her for another woman, it would undoubtedly give Sarah's ego a pretty good drubbing, but it surely wouldn't break her heart. Hell, it might not even break her stride. That was the whole point of marrying Warren, after all.

But a man like Nick Chiara…?

Oh, brother. Sarah didn't even want to think about all the hearts he'd probably broken. Nor did she want to think about the fact that as a widower, his own heart had likely been shattered several years ago when his wife passed away.

While she was cursing and trying not to think about the man who'd just unsettled her so, it occurred to Sarah that she'd probably turned in the wrong direction after hustling down the palace steps. She should have turned left, but instead she'd gone right. Or was it the reverse?

Just ahead of her, she saw a stone bench beside another one of the palace's many fountains. This one appeared to be a chubby marble Cupid with his bow tightly drawn and his arrow aimed directly at the moon. Maybe if she sat for a moment she could get her bearings. As if she'd had any for the past twelve hours or so.

Plopping down on the bench, Sarah smoothed out and arranged the vast satin yardage of her skirt in front of her. In the moonlight, its color was less a vivid red than a rich and wine-drenched burgundy. She reached down and edged back the hemline in order to peek at her toes in the silver sandals. Their thin, metallic leather straps glittered almost magically.

"Weren't you supposed to lose one of those slippers on the palace stairs, Cinderella?"

Much to Sarah's amazement, she recognized Sir Dominic Chiara's voice after hearing it only a few times. It was a deep, rich baritone, now touched by an Italian accent, now tinged by some kind of private amusement. Solid. Sure. Sexy. It sent a cascade of chills down her spine.

"If Cinderella's shoes had been this tight, her fairy tale would have ended at midnight," she answered, slipping off one of the sandals and reaching down to rub her foot.

"Well, then, thank heaven for loose shoes."

"Mmm," Sarah murmured. "None of this was my idea, Sir Dominic. Your aunt was the one playing fairy godmother tonight."

"Doesn't surprise me," he said with a chuckle. "May I join you?"

"Won't they miss you at the palace?"

"Probably. It doesn't matter."

Sarah moved her skirt to make room for him on

the little bench. His shoulder was warm against her bare arm. Moonlight glanced off the tips of his polished shoes while a faint breeze wafted his aftershave in her direction. He smelled divine. Citrus and sandalwood and something very intensely male. She almost didn't want to speak, but rather just sit here inhaling his scent.

Still, Sarah had never been known for her ability to maintain silence. Especially when she was nervous. Her mind tended to race. It was going about ninety miles an hour at the moment. In circles.

"How did you win it?" she asked.

"Excuse me?"

"Your bronze medal."

"Oh. That." He pointed toward the fountain that was gently splashing in front of their bench. "Just like our friend over there," he said.

Sarah blinked and then stared at the pudgy marble statue. "You won a medal for playing Cupid?"

"Archery, Ms. Hunter." He laughed softly. "It's an ancient and much revered sport in Montebello, something every schoolboy learns as soon as he's tall enough to hold a bow."

Playing Cupid! She felt like slapping herself up the side of her head. How stupid could she be? He probably thought she could win a medal for being dense. It was just that he smelled so good, and the warmth from his black sleeve was seeping into her, and she was so jet-lagged that she couldn't think straight.

"Archery. Of course. You must have learned very well."

"Well enough," he said. "That was a long time ago."

"That will be nice for you and Leo," she said then as her mind went skipping ahead again.

"What will be nice?"

"You'll teach him to use a bow and arrow, won't you, when he's tall enough?"

"Perhaps."

His voice drifted off a bit sadly, reminding Sarah of the reason she was in Montebello in the first place. She wasn't Cinderella, after all, here to linger in the moonlight with Prince Charming. She was a psychologist and this man's son was her patient.

She wondered why Dr. Chiara had been so reluctant about getting help for the child. Earlier, she'd assumed it was because the man was elderly and indifferent. Now she knew that wasn't true. His concern for the boy was evident in the tone of his voice. She tilted her head in his direction and witnessed the dark distress on his handsome face. She made herself focus on the distress. Not on the sculpture of his nose or the strong line of his jaw. Not on the way the moonlight picked out silver threads at his temples. Especially not on the obsidian shine of his black eyes.

"Leo will speak again," she said. "I'm sure of it. And I don't think it will take long. I have every confidence that I can help your son, Dr. Chiara."

"Really?" There was a dubious note in his voice, and then he sighed with just a hint of indulgence. "How long have you been in the nanny business, Ms. Hunter?"

The nanny business. Sarah shook her head. This really wasn't going to work.

"Well, that's just it..."

She drew in her lower lip, sinking her eyeteeth into it, debating whether or not to blow her cover this early, to risk Sir Dominic's anger, to do exactly what the king had told her not to do. Well, what could happen? King Marcus wasn't going to throw her in a dungeon. He wasn't going to yell "Off with her head." And her instincts told her that, even if Dr. Chiara were angry, he wouldn't prevent her from helping his son.

When it came right down to it, she just wasn't a good liar. It went against everything she believed in. And she'd never been any good at keeping secrets, which was why nobody in her family ever told her anything.

She glared at the wet Cupid, glistening under the silvery waters of the fountain. "Just shoot me," she muttered.

"I beg your pardon?"

"I'm not exactly in the nanny business, Sir Dominic.'' She drew in a breath, a deep one to fuel her confession. ''I'm supposed to pretend to be a nanny so you won't throw me out of the house before I've been able to work with your son. This was the king's idea. And Lady Satherwaite's, too.''

He merely gazed at her, fixed her with those ebony eyes, while Sarah gulped in more air and continued.

''The king and your aunt were frustrated, I believe, by what they perceived as your lack of action, and they felt they had to do something before Leo's condition became worse. So the king prevailed upon my father, his longtime friend, and my father prevailed upon me.''

Sir Dominic was staring at her now, hard, terribly silent, a rather bemused expression on his face. Sarah took another deep breath and pressed on.

''Well, actually, my father did more than prevail. He sort of kidnapped me and tossed me on a royal jet, I think it was yesterday, but, you know, my mind's sort of fried at this point, so it could have been the day before. And, well...''

She threw up her hands, then let them drop in her lap. There was really nothing more to say, except...

''Here I am.''

There she was, indeed.

Nick had never in his life, in all of his thirty-six years, heard a speech that picked up speed and intensity in direct proportion to its loss of coherence.

He didn't know whether this woman was delirious or demented or simply delightful.

He didn't know whether he was angry because she had lied, or elated because she had told the truth.

The only thing he knew was that he wanted her. Despite the fact that he hardly knew her. Despite the fact that he wasn't sure if he even liked her. Despite everything.

He wanted her.

Whoever this Sarah Hunter was. Whatever she was. Wherever she had come from.

He wanted her.

The feeling was so astonishing, so visceral, and took Nick by such surprise that he actually found himself glancing toward the fountain to make sure that Cupid's pointed arrow was still there, drawn and poised against the arc of the bow.

Amazingly enough, it was.

Chapter 6

The next morning, Nick slept in—something he hadn't done since medical school. There was no alarm to wake him, no frantic call from the hospital, no shrill beeper to wrench him from sleep.

What finally awakened him a little after nine o'clock was a bright peal of laughter drifting through his open window. By the time he opened his eyes, he was already smiling. By the time he had showered and shaved and dressed, the grin was plastered on his face and he thought he must look like a fool.

He probably was a fool, he decided.

And somehow he didn't care.

It was good to feel completely alive, to feel revitalized. It was as if his blood count had been off the past five years, and suddenly he could feel the missing vitamins and minerals coursing through his arteries.

Minerals, mostly.

Iron.

Good God. He hadn't been this hard in years.

He was still wearing the remnants of a grin when he walked out onto the terrace.

"There you are, darling," his aunt exclaimed. "I was only moments away from sending someone in to take your pulse. It isn't like you, Nicky, to sleep so late."

"I'm on vacation." He kissed the top of her head. As far back as he could remember, Honoria's hair had smelled like lavender. It was no different this morning. She was dressed in lavender, as well, he noticed. Acres of it. With miles of colorful beads draped around her neck and dangling from her wrists. As much as his aunt teased him about being descended from pirates, he was fairly certain there was at least one gypsy up the maternal side of his family tree.

"Coffee or tea, dear?" she asked as he pulled out the chair across from hers.

"Coffee, please."

While she filled a cup for him, Nick gazed around the terrace. There was a stone wall on its southern edge where the palace grounds began their perilous and rocky slope down to the sea. He always worried about Leo out here despite the fact that his son was agile as a cat and surefooted as any mountain goat.

"Where's Leo?" he asked, taking the cup and saucer from his aunt. "I thought I heard the nanny laughing just a few moments ago."

"You did. She's a delightful creature. I think the two of them have wandered off in search of his tricycle."

He had already decided not to confront his aunt with the truth he'd learned about Sarah Hunter last night. Much as he hated deception of any sort, he couldn't help but appreciate the little gleam in Honoria Satherwaite's eyes or the heightened color of her ancient cheeks. Let the old girl think she was putting one over on him, he decided. Let her have a little fun. What would it hurt?

"I've decided not to insist you fire the nanny," he said after a sip of the hot, strong Arabica.

"Well, I should hope not," she answered with a snort. "She dotes on Leo, and I daresay the child feels the same. They seem to have bonded. Instantly."

"Good."

Like father, like son, he thought, once more feeling his lips quirking in something like a besotted smile.

"Are you feeling all right, dear?" His aunt was looking at him rather strangely.

"Yes. Quite."

She continued to peruse his face. "You look a bit queasy. Were you out terribly late last night?"

"Not late at all. In fact—"

Just then his son came roaring around the side of the cottage, doing a perfect wheelie on his blue-and-yellow plastic trike. Thank God for helmets, Nick thought.

Sarah Hunter wasn't far behind. In a white T-shirt, a pair of khaki shorts and sneakers, she was even more delectable than she'd been the night before in her designer gown. Just as moonlight had become her, so did daylight.

The sun picked up some reddish highlights in her wavy hair and warmed her skin tones to a golden hue. She looked young and vibrant and healthy as a horse. He felt a cautious little tic in the vicinity of his heart, knowing all too well how deceptive disease could be, how insidious illness was, how even the young and vibrant weren't immune.

Leo circled the table, his little legs punishing the trike's pedals, while the nanny sauntered forward, lifting a hand to rake back her hair.

"Good morning," she said, her voice as bright and warm as the sunshine itself.

"Good morning." Nick pushed back his chair and stood. "Won't you join us for coffee, Ms. Hunter?"

"No, thanks. I've already had two cups. Any more and you'd be able to see my synapses sizzle."

She laughed, and once again Nick heard the sound

to which he'd awakened, the music that had turned
him on so. Damned if it wasn't happening again with
an unsyncopated rhythm in his chest and a decided
quickening in his groin.

"How goes the jet lag, dear?" Aunt Honoria inquired. "You look quite acclimated to me. Doesn't
she, Nicky?"

"Acclimated," he murmured, resuming his seat
rather than flaunt his unbidden, unanticipated, unpar-
alleled erection. "Yes, she looks very acclimated."

"I think I'm recovering," she said. "I'm feeling
much better. All I really needed, I guess, was a good
night's sleep."

So, she'd slept well after their moonlit stroll back
to the cottage. He'd shrugged out of his jacket at
some point and placed it around her shoulders as they
walked. He'd held her hand when their path had led
them around the wet pavement of a particularly en-
ergetic fountain. He'd reveled in the sound of her
laughter and he'd thought about kissing her good-
night. Actually, he'd thought about far more than that
while he was trying to fall asleep.

But apparently Sarah had slept well. What had he
expected, after all? That the woman would have
tossed and turned for hours, thinking about him as
he had thought about her?

Well… Actually, yes. That wasn't such an out-
landish wish. It wasn't as if women hadn't lost sleep
over him before. Wasn't it just yesterday he'd been

complaining about the unwanted attentions of the fairer sex? What about the royal appointments secretary? He wouldn't be surprised if Sophia Strezzi had gone to bed with his bronze medal around her neck last night.

Feeling slightly churlish, Nick reached out to snag Leo on his tenth circuit of the table. He lifted the boy off the trike and settled him on his lap, hugging Leo tightly and pressing his lips against his son's soft warm hair.

"How's my boy this morning? You slept well, Leo, I'll bet. What shall we do today?"

Naturally, Leo didn't answer. But his nanny piped up loud and clear.

"Well, actually, Leo and I were planning on a few hours of play with some of the toys I brought him from America," she said. "At least until lunch."

The way her green eyes fixed firmly on his, and from the tone of her voice, Nick knew immediately what Sarah Hunter meant. The playtime wouldn't be what it appeared. Not to Leo, at least. And the toys wouldn't be merely random playthings, but rather a variety of diagnostic tools. He kept forgetting she wasn't really a nanny.

"I think that's a marvelous idea," his aunt said, obviously catching on to her intentions. "And it's such a lovely day, I wouldn't mind going for a walk, Nicky. You'll join me, won't you?"

A walk? This from the woman whose idea of rig-

orous exercise was pouring tea and passing a plate
of scones, mostly in her own direction. A walk? Had
he heard her right? Lady Honoria Satherwaite called
for a car to take her to the palace, which was less
than a quarter mile away. How many times had he
heard her say "Why walk when you can ride, darling?"

She really did want him out of the way so the
therapy could begin. Perhaps it was just as well.

"Of course, I'll join you," he said, wondering if
it would upset his aunt unduly if he wore a stethoscope and carried a portable oxygen unit, just in case.

Sarah went to her room to gather the toys she'd
tossed into her suitcase, wishing her father had given
her a bit of a warning so that she could have picked
up a few more items from her office at the clinic,
where she had a huge collection of dolls, ranging
from stuffed cotton forms with the mere suggestion
of features, all the way to a family of anatomically
correct figures.

She'd make do, of course. She always did.

It wasn't the play therapy equipment that made a
good child therapist, after all. It was the ability to
observe a patient interacting *with* the equipment, and
the ability to correctly interpret those interactions.
The practice of child psychotherapy was as much art
as it was science. That was even more true in the

case of a mute patient, a child who offered no verbal clues whatsoever.

How she wished she could magically transport little Leo to the clinic in San Francisco. She realized that she'd probably become very spoiled by the two-way mirror in her office that allowed her to observe without interfering, and by the video equipment that enabled her to focus exclusively on the patient during a session without being distracted by the constant taking of notes. The videos also allowed her to review behaviors, to pick up on subtleties she might have missed during the session itself.

She grabbed three soft-sculptured dolls and a small bag of bright wooden blocks, along with a spiral sketch book and a box of crayons. Deciding she'd merely observe this first time, Sarah didn't bother with her notebook or a pen. As for a tape recorder, what good would it do to listen to the sound of her own voice when it was Leo's voice that was important?

But silent or not, she could already tell that young Leo Chiara was a very bright kid. One who would immediately know the difference between a playful nanny and a therapist in disguise. She and Leo seemed to have a good rapport so far—a boy and his nanny—and Sarah meant to keep it that way.

As for her rapport with Leo's father... She'd thought about that plenty the night before, and she'd undoubtedly think about it later. But right now she had work to do, so she pushed any notions about Sir Dominic to the farthest reaches of her brain. It wasn't often that thoughts of life outside her work vied for her attention during therapy sessions, and she resented that intrusion now. He was just a gorgeous man, after all. In the grand scheme of her life, that didn't count for much.

The child was in his room, watching cartoons on a small portable TV. It may have been a room in a cottage on the palace grounds in Montebello, but it was still a kid's room with a rumpled bunk bed and the usual clutter. The TV was on the floor, and like most kids, Leo sat cross-legged, barely a foot from the screen.

"I like your television, Leo," Sarah said, kneeling on the floor behind him. "It's very different from mine. Can you show me how it works? What do you press to turn it on and off?" She pointed to a button, clearly labeled contrast. "Here?"

Bless his little guy heart, the boy went right for the proper switch and turned the TV off. As soon as the screen went dark, Sarah tossed out her bevy of toys onto the floor beside him

"Look what I've got," she said.

He looked.

"You can play with anything you'd like, Leo."

He looked some more, and then he reached for the largest of the cotton doll figures.

Sarah sat back, smiling, feeling enormously

pleased that her young patient had chosen the human form over the inanimate blocks and crayons. It was a good sign, a further clue that little Leo, even though he wasn't speaking, hadn't completely withdrawn from interaction with humanity.

While he perused the largest doll, fashioned out of a dark blue denim fabric, the expression on Leo's face seemed fairly neutral. No fear, anger or apprehension registered on his features, as far as Sarah could tell. Then, when he reached out for the smallest of the dolls, a little flicker of a smile played at the edges of his lips. He inspected both of the stuffed dolls, walked them across a foot of carpet, bent them to sit side by side against his outstretched leg.

Longing dreadfully for her trusty video cam, Sarah found herself taking quick mental notes. The three graduated dolls, of course, though they were featureless, could easily be taken for father, mother and child. It was interesting that to this point Leo had ignored the midsize figure. Of course, he'd never known his mother, so perhaps that shouldn't be so surprising.

She watched him interact with the father and child figures for the next several minutes. His demeanor was calm enough. In fact, young Leo, though silent, appeared to be thoroughly enjoying himself.

So far, so good.

If she were home, if she were going to be working on a long-term basis with a patient, Sarah wouldn't

have intervened at all. She would have let the play
therapy take its own course. But—dammit—considering that she only had a few weeks to work with
Leo, she felt forced to hurry the process along. The
child deserved better, but what could she do under
the circumstances? It was clearly a case of Sarah's
concentrated help or no help at all.

"We could pretend," she said, her tone light and
full of enthusiasm. "We could pretend that these are
real people, Leo. That might be fun. Maybe we could
make up a story about them. Or act out a play. I
wonder which one is the man." Again she was careful not to ask the boy a direct question.

Without hesitation, Leo picked up the largest doll
and handed it to Sarah with a smile.

"I think you're right," she said. "He's very tall.
And probably strong as well. Which one is the child,
I wonder? It might be fun to have a little boy in our
story."

It was hardly a surprise to Sarah when the child
gave her the smallest doll.

"Hmm," she murmured, gazing around before
reaching for the third doll, trying not to be too obvious, intensely aware that she was rushing the session, but believing she had no other choice.

"Well, let's see. We've got a man for our story,
and we've got a boy, as well. Now, I wonder who
could this be?"

She lay the three dolls in a row on the floor between them. Crossing her arms, she drew in her lower lip and made a humming sound, as if trying to decide who the new, middle-size character was, and hoping that the boy would provide her some sort of clue.

He gave her a clue, all right. Leo snatched up the middle-size doll and threw it across the room, where it landed on a pile of clothes at the bottom of his closet. Then he jumped up, raced to the closet and slammed the door.

After that, while Sarah watched without comment, he came back, propped the other two dolls in front of him, turned on the TV, and pretended his nanny wasn't there.

Well, that was probably enough therapy for one day, Sarah decided. And so much for the simple fairy tale of Mama Bear and Papa Bear and Baby Bear.

This wasn't going to be easy by any means.

Just who was the woman in the closet?

"Would you like to sit for a moment, love?" Nick asked his aunt as they paused in front of the burnt-out guest cottage where Desmond Caruso had met his untimely but not altogether unpredictable end a few weeks ago.

"I don't think so, dear."

The woman continually amazed him. He'd thought the walk would do her in after a mere hundred yards or so, but Honoria Satherwaite was still steaming ahead like a great ship, not even breathing hard, despite her disdain for exercise and her excessive tonnage, increased this morning by at least five pounds of beads spilling over her ample bosom and rattling on her wrists.

"Our nanny was inquiring at breakfast about the fire," she said as she gazed in the direction of the ruined cottage. "I don't believe Ms. Hunter knows anything about the murder. Unless you happened to mention it to her last night."

Nick shook his head. "No reason to mention it," he replied. "We walked home by another path. I thought the sight of this place might depress her."

"It is depressing, isn't it, dear?" She clucked her tongue softly. "I do wish they'd catch the culprit. Although I imagine the authorities aren't lacking for suspects. I wasn't able to tell them a thing since I was in London with you that night."

He'd had a devil of a time convincing Honoria to attend a British medical conference with him, believing it would probably be the last time she'd ever see her native city. It turned out to have been a terrible idea because the majority of her old schoolmates and first cousins were dead, and his aunt spent her time there feeling like some sort of prehistoric human artifact.

"Well, even if we'd been here, I doubt either one of us could have been of much help to the police. I told them what little I could about his medical history."

"I didn't realize you had treated him," she said, sounding only slightly surprised as she continued to gaze at the badly scorched wall of the guest house.

"I treated him on a few occasions. Never for anything serious. There was nothing I could tell them that appeared to interest the police one way or another."

He didn't bother to add that the reason Desmond Caruso had consulted him a few times in the past few years was for venereal diseases. Luckily for Caruso, they'd all been curable. Aunt Honoria would undoubtedly enjoy the gossip, but now that the poor man was dead, it wouldn't do to sully his reputation any more than it had been while he was alive.

"It's unfortunate that none of us was able to help the investigators. Leo and Estella were here when it happened, of course." His aunt referred to Leo's previous nanny. "But Estella insisted that she didn't see or hear anything untoward, and that Leo slept quite soundly through all of the commotion."

"You aren't afraid, are you, love?" Nick asked. "About a murderer being on the loose?"

"Heavens no." She waved a dismissive ringed-and-beaded hand. "I can think of at least a dozen people who'd have quite happily done Desmond in. The police believe his murder was an isolated incident, and I completely agree. Don't you, dear?"

"I'm sure it was." Nick looked at his watch. "Do you suppose Leo and his nanny have had ample time to get acquainted by now? Shall we go back?"

"Yes, dear," she said, patting his hand. "I believe we've been gone quite long enough."

Nick ignored the devious little smile that worked its way across the old girl's lips.

Sarah was in the kitchen, doing her damndest to fix Leo a peanut butter and jelly sandwich with some weird Italian brand of peanut butter that was way too runny and a jar of Lady Satherwaite's English orange marmalade.

"I wouldn't mind having one of those," Nick Chiara said from the doorway.

"Sure."

She reached for two more slices of bread and tried to ignore the fact that her heart was suddenly doing jumping jacks in her chest and her knees felt like Silly Putty. What was wrong with her? Never had the mere presence of a male discombobulated her so. Not even that slender, young, blond god, Billy Dean, in fourth grade.

It was one thing to get all weak-kneed and gooey when you were ten years old. But Sarah was almost thirty. This was just ludicrous. It was insane. Whatever Sir Dominic was doing to her, she wanted him to stop it right now. Immediately. Permanently. Even retroactively, to include last night.

She stuck a knife in the peanut butter jar and slathered some on a slice of bread.

"How did this morning go?" he asked, all the way in the kitchen now, crossing his arms and leaning one of those lean, jean-clad hips against the counter.

Grateful to get her mind back on a professional track, Sarah replied, "It went very well. Actually, it was pretty interesting."

He raised a dark eyebrow. "How so?"

Sarah reached for the marmalade jar and spooned some of the sticky yellow stuff onto another slice of bread. "I'd like to ask you some questions about the women in Leo's life."

"All right," he said, shifting his stance against the counter. "Ask away."

She paused a moment, carefully framing her question. "Other than your aunt, are there any other females who've come into more than mere casual contact with the boy? Nannies, for instance. Or other caregivers. A baby-sitter, maybe, or a housekeeper or even a cook. Perhaps even some of your close female friends. Women who might have spent time with him."

"Nannies," he replied. "A succession of them, I'm afraid, in the past four years. Seems they always run off and get married."

"What about teachers or other caretakers? Does your son attend any sort of preschool or day care?"

He shook his head. "That isn't as common in

Montebello as it seems to be in the States. As far as I know, Leo never spent much time with the housekeeper or the cook.''

''What about other females?''

What Sarah meant by ''other females'' was Sir Dominic's girlfriends, but she didn't quite know how to put the question, and she didn't want to sound personally curious rather than professionally interested. But there had to be women in his life. A flock. A whole herd. The ice maiden, Sophia Strezzi, was undoubtedly just the chilly tip of a very large iceberg.

''Other females?'' he echoed.

For a moment, Sarah wasn't sure if he truly didn't understand her, or if the man was merely being coy or perhaps even chivalrous, not wanting to mention other women in the presence of a possible conquest.

Conquest? Where had that thought come from? Since when had she started thinking of herself as a conquest? Sarah wondered. Maybe it was his cologne or aftershave that was scrambling her brain. It was probably too late to fall back on the old jet lag excuse.

''Friends of yours, Sir Dominic. Lady friends. Female companions. Dates. I'm guessing a man in your position… Well…'' She shrugged almost helplessly. ''You know.''

What did she have to do? Paint him an erotic picture? Make obscene gestures with her hands?

''There's no one,'' he said.

"No one at the moment, you mean."

"There's no one at all. I haven't had a female companion or even a date since my wife died."

"Oh."

Sarah wasn't sure exactly what she meant by that rather breathless little *Oh*. Sadness or surprise or a sudden quickening of her interest. All those emotions, she supposed. The quickening, mostly. Definitely. The quickening.

He shoved away from the counter and came a little closer. "Unless, of course, you count our date last night, Ms. Hunter."

Her heart felt like a yo-yo, dropping to her stomach then jumping up in her throat. Sarah stuck the spoon back in the marmalade jar and dumped another heaping of the sticky stuff on the bread.

"I wouldn't count last night, Sir Dominic," she said.

"Nick," he said softly.

He was close enough now that she could feel his breath on her nick. Her *neck*. God.

"I'm glad you're here, Sarah," he said, lifting a lock of her hair. "And not just for my son's sake."

All right. Whoa. Hold the phone. She *was* here for his son's sake. Period.

Sarah was about to tell him exactly that when Lady Satherwaite screamed.

Chapter 7

Sir Dominic rushed out of the kitchen so fast that Sarah was surprised he hadn't won a gold medal for sprinting in addition to his bronze for archery. By the time she had dropped the sticky slice of bread in her hand and raced around the corner into the living room, Nick was already kneeling, attending to his aunt, who was flat on the floor in the middle of the room.

Well, not exactly flat, Sarah couldn't help but notice. A mountainous heap was more like it.

"How bloody stupid of me," the prone Lady Satherwaite wailed, batting away her nephew's hands and attempting to lever her great weight up from the floor.

Thank God the woman didn't appear to be badly injured, Sarah thought, even as she was picturing a huge, lavender whale—a rather indignant one—beached on the sand-colored carpet.

"Don't move, Aunt Honoria," Nick said sternly. His gaze flicked up to Sarah. "Will you bring me the telephone from the kitchen, please. Hurry."

By the time Sarah dashed back with the portable phone in her hand, Nick had a pillow wedged beneath his aunt's head and he was taking her pulse while Lady Satherwaite continued to berate both herself and her nephew.

"Nicky, darling, I'd much rather get up, if you don't mind. It's quite drafty down here on the floor. Not to mention uncomfortable and damned embarrassing."

"Hush," he told her, keeping his eyes fixed on his watch while he gripped her wrist.

When he let go of her hand, apparently satisfied that her pulse was all right, Sarah spoke up. "Would you like me to call an emergency number Sir Dominic? Do you use 9-1-1 in Montebello?"

"I'll call the hospital directly," he said, reaching up for the phone. "It will be faster. Thanks."

His dark gaze lingered on Sarah's face a moment, adding silent thanks to those he'd expressed.

"I certainly hope you aren't calling for an ambulance, Nicky," Lady Satherwaite snapped. "I don't want one."

"I don't care what you want, love," he said, allowing himself to smile down at her just a bit as he punched in a series of numbers on the telephone. "You're going to the hospital, and that's that."

"Oh, piddle," she said.

"Hush."

While Nick was issuing quiet commands into the telephone, Sarah knelt down to see if she could be of any help to his aunt.

"Is there anything I can do?" she asked, readjusting the pillow beneath her head. "Would you like a glass of water, Lady Satherwaite?"

"Just see to my boys while I'm incapacitated, will you, dear? Both of them. Leo *and* Nicky."

"Yes, of course, I will," Sarah assured her. "You don't even have to ask."

Lady Satherwaite raised her hand without any apparent difficulty and smiled as she patted Sarah's cheek.

"There's a good girl," she said. "I knew I could depend on you, Sarah dear. I knew it from the very first moment I laid eyes on you."

After that, rather than wait for the ambulance to arrive, Sarah had excused herself and gone into Leo's bedroom, hoping to keep the child occupied while his great aunt was being tended to in the living room. She'd been relieved to see that Leo was still so entranced by the cartoon on the television, apparently he hadn't even been aware of the commotion outside his door.

Sarah settled on the floor beside him, then proceeded to turn up the volume on the TV just a bit in order to drown out the sound of the ambulance's arrival and departure as she was still operating on the theory that the boy's self-imposed silence was the result of trauma of some sort.

The poor kid certainly didn't need anything else to upset him. There was no way of predicting how he would react to it.

Finally, after the ambulance left and when Leo appeared to be becoming bored with the cartoons, Sarah said, "I feel like going for a walk. It's such a pretty day. I'd love it if you'd come with me, Leo, and keep me from getting lost. I still don't know my way around the palace grounds very well."

He nodded, then jumped up from the floor with a surprising amount of enthusiasm.

"Great!" Sarah clapped her hands. "You'll need to put some shoes on. I bet they're in your closet."

The moment the words were out of her mouth she realized her mistake, because also in his closet was the doll he'd slammed in there earlier. She'd been remiss in not retrieving the plaything. Chalk up another mistake to being distracted by Nick Chiara.

"Why don't I just get the shoes for you?" she suggested, heading quickly toward the closet door, then opening it just enough to reach in and grope blindly for his little sneakers. When her fingers brushed across the doll, she poked it farther down in a bundle of clothes, intending to come back and get it later.

She watched Leo tug on a pair of socks before he put on the sneakers. She tied the laces for him, unable to resist the little instructional drama of the rabbit going into his den as she made the loops. He laughed. Soundlessly. Then she took his hand and walked him toward the front door.

Once outside, Sarah turned to her right, toward the palace. There were so many fountains along this path, and she was hoping to get Leo to do some happy, even therapeutic splashing. Maybe she would even be able to locate the chubby Cupid from the night before to see if he appeared as magical by day as he did by night.

She'd only taken a few steps when Leo tugged her in the opposite direction.

Tugging back gently, she said, "Let's go this way. We can play in the fountains."

He shook his head.

"Please," Sarah said.

He shook his head again. Harder.

"Pretty please with sugar on top."

This time the little boy shook his head so vigorously that Sarah was surprised he didn't knock himself out. He stamped his foot, as well. The combined gestures were probably the loudest, most adamant *no* that a silent child could muster.

"Okay. Okay. You win." Sarah sighed as she gazed down the path to the left. West, wasn't it? South? Oh, hell. What difference did it make? Lost would be lost, regardless of the direction.

"We'll go your way, Leo. I just hope we can find a fountain or two." Not to mention finding our way back home, she added a bit mournfully to herself.

As it turned out, there were probably more fountains on this part of the palace grounds than there were behind them. Sarah and Leo walked past a life-size pair of rearing bronze horses, their wet hooves glistening in the sunlight. Farther along the path, there were marble angels, cherubim and seraphim with placid faces and big, dripping wings. A little way beyond the angels stood an ugly satyr with hairy legs and cloven feet, playing his panpipe or whatever it was that satyrs played, under a cascade of water.

Finally, they came to a lovely fountain presided over by a gentle Saint Francis of Assisi with a bird perched on each of his gracefully outstretched hands. There were rainbows in the rising and falling arcs of water all around him. It was beautiful, peaceful, a perfect fountain for a little boy to splash around in.

Leo appeared to agree because when she suggested it, he immediately plucked off his shoes and socks and made a beeline for the water. Sarah sat on a scrolled stone bench just a few yards away and watched, thinking that perhaps tomorrow or the next day, she and Leo could come here again with a picnic lunch. Maybe they could convince his father to come along. Well, maybe that wasn't such a good idea, considering the man's distraction quotient.

They'd only been there for a few minutes when a woman approached the fountain. A rather odd woman, Sarah decided. She was about sixty years old, give or take a few years, with her gray hair in a soft bob that framed her narrow face and gave her a kind of mouselike appearance. In fact, the closer the little woman came, the mousier she looked. She even moved like a mouse, scurrying rather than simply walking. Her gaze darted around her in all directions.

Leo stopped splashing in the bright water and stared at the woman as she approached. Sarah noticed that it was the same, rather peculiar way the child had given her the once-over yesterday when they'd first met, scrutinizing her face as if he'd been trying with all his young might to identify her.

Apparently he didn't recognize the mouse person, though, because he quickly resumed stomping in the water under the outstretched arms of Saint Francis.

"My goodness! Aren't you a brave young woman!" she said by way of a greeting. There was even a tiny squeak in her voice, and her accent sounded vaguely British.

"Hello," Sarah said.

The woman looked behind her, over her shoulder,

and then back at Sarah. "Aren't you worried, young lady? Aren't you just a little bit afraid?"

Oh, boy. Sarah detected a faint whiff of paranoia now. She started to wonder if somehow she and Leo had strayed onto the grounds of the local looney bin.

"Afraid of what?" she asked.

The nervous little woman slid onto the bench beside her, leaned close and whispered. "Not afraid of *what,* young lady. Afraid of *whom!* The murderer, or murderess as the case may be. This is my very first time out and about since it happened."

"Since what happened?" Sarah felt as if she were playing Twenty Questions.

The woman looked around again, a full three hundred and sixty worried degrees. Her voice got even lower, and her squeak turned into a croak when she said, "The murder."

She turned her gaze toward Leo now, who was happily stomping in front of Saint Francis. "Isn't that the little Chiara boy? Sir Dominic's son?"

"Yes."

"You must be his nanny, then?"

Sarah nodded.

"Well, then, surely you know all about the crime last month. It happened practically next door to Sir Dominic's house."

"Oh. You mean the fire," Sarah said.

"That, too. One assumes the blaze was set in order to cover up the murder."

There'd been a murder? Somebody had been murdered in the burnt guest cottage? Sophia Strezzi hadn't said anything about that when they passed the place yesterday, had she? Sarah wondered. Surely she'd have remembered any mention of a death or a murder, especially considering that the possible trauma of the fire was one of her theories about Leo's problem. Now the possibilities of trauma seemed to have increased immeasurably.

"Who was murdered?" she asked, lowering her voice so Leo wouldn't overhear the conversation.

After another sweeping, nervous scan of her surroundings, the woman leaned closer and whispered, "The victim was Desmond Caruso. The bastard nephew of the king. Bashed over the head quite brutally, I'm told. It was terrible."

"And they haven't caught the killer yet? They don't even know who it was?"

"No. At least I don't believe so. I look in the paper every day. He could be watching us right now, you know. Or she. It's horrid. Just terrible. I live alone, and I haven't been able to sleep a single wink since that awful night. And I only dared to venture out today after seeing you and the child out here, both of you looking so very brave and unconcerned."

Sarah didn't feel so very brave and unconcerned anymore. Why hadn't anyone told her this before? Why did everyone seem to assume that because Leo was only five years old, he couldn't possibly be affected by such grisly events? Now, learning that a murder had accompanied the fire, Sarah was even more convinced that those events had something to do with Leo's silence.

As soon as Nick returned from the hospital, she was going to be on him about this subject like white on rice. Not only as it related to Leo's condition, but because she mightily resented the fact that no one had thought it important to let her know that there was a murderer on the loose.

Her benchmate was actually trembling now.

"Oh, dear. I've come this far," the woman said, "but now I'm afraid to walk home all by myself. I wonder, young lady... Would you? Could you accompany me?"

"Yes, of course."

All of a sudden, now that she knew there was a murderer on the loose, Sarah wasn't all that crazy about being out here either. She called to Leo to get his shoes on.

By the time she and Leo had walked the frightened Mrs. Ratigan back to her house adjacent to the palace grounds—Sarah had almost laughed out loud when the mousey little woman actually introduced herself by that name—and then retraced their steps back to the Chiara's residence, it was well into the afternoon.

Sarah was starving. Poor Leo, she had to assume,

was starving, as well. She wasn't exactly winning any awards in the nanny department, was she?

While he disappeared into the bathroom, Sarah raced into his room to retrieve the doll hidden in the closet. She tossed it into her own room, closed the door, and then headed for the kitchen.

She wasn't exactly winning any awards in the psychotherapist department either, she thought, as she washed her hands in the kitchen sink. Other than discovering that Leo had an intense reaction to the middle-size doll, she really hadn't learned anything else about his mutism, except possibly for Mrs Ratigan's account of the nearby fire and murder.

But who knew if that was even true? Maybe the woman made a habit of accosting people and scaring them with tales of murder and mayhem on the palace grounds. Maybe it was just her way of having a bit of fun with visitors to the palace. Who knew?

It was interesting the way Leo had so closely scrutinized Mrs. Ratigan when she'd approached. Sarah recalled that they passed several men on their walk this morning, but Leo hadn't paid particular attention to any of them. There was definitely some female aspect to his problem that needed delving into.

Right now, though, she needed to delve into their lunch. And before she did that, she was going to have to clean up the bread and marmalade that she'd dropped earlier before running to Lady Satherwaite's assistance. Sarah didn't know much about physics, but she did know it was an immutable law that bread always fell butter- or jelly-side down. What a mess.

She picked up the partial sandwich, pitched it in the trash, then reached for a paper towel and bent down to swab up the sticky marmalade and crumbs. Just as she was making a second pass over the spot with the towel, Sarah felt something—a huge, hot hand—clamp on her backside. She was so startled she nearly went head first into the cabinet under the sink. Shrieking.

She stood up and whirled around to confront her attacker.

"*Aiee. Scusa,* signorina. Pardon me."

The man who spoke looked even more startled than Sarah. He was young—in his early twenties. His dark brown hair was long and sun-streaked, and he wore a Hard Rock Café T-shirt and a pair of ragged cutoffs. Surely not a murderer, she thought, much to her immediate relief. He looked more like a Montebellan surfer.

"Who are you? How did you get in here?" she asked, not knowing whether he understood English or not.

"Through the door," he answered in slow and careful English, pointing to the door that led to the terrace. "I am Bruno. I come to see Estella."

"Estella? There's no one here by that name."

"She is the nanny. Here." He gestured around the

kitchen. "Estella is the nanny to the bambino who lives here. Leo."

"Well, maybe she was," Sarah said. "But not anymore. I'm the new nanny."

He looked incredibly disappointed, almost as if he were about to cry. "Is true?"

"Yes. I'm afraid so. There's no Estella here."

"Aiee."

He pulled out a chair and sat, as if he were quite comfortable in the Chiara kitchen. As if he'd been here many times before. Sarah made a mental note to find out more about this Estella, the nanny who'd preceded her.

"I was away," Bruno said rather mournfully. "I did not know Estella would not be here when I come back. Where did she go?"

"I'm sorry. I don't know."

He dug in the pocket of his cutoffs, coming up with a tiny box, which he carefully opened. "You see. I bring her this."

Sarah gazed at the diamond ring, whose stone was hardly bigger than a flea. The poor guy. Even though he'd almost scared her to death, Sarah felt sympathetic.

"I'm sorry," she said again. "I don't know where she is."

"Aiee." He dragged his fingers through his hair. "Maybe the bambino knows where. Leo. Maybe we

ask him. Tell him it is Bruno wanting to find Estella.''

"I'm sure he doesn't know," Sarah told him. Obviously the young man hadn't seen Leo since the boy had stopped speaking. "Perhaps I can ask Dr. Chiara or his aunt about Estella. They might know her address."

His face brightened a bit as he stood up. "Yes, they might know address. You ask, please."

"I'll ask them later this evening," she said.

"Okay. Okay. I come back tomorrow, yes? You will have address for me?''

"I'll do my best," she said.

"Best. Yes." He extended his hand. "I am sorry about…'' His dark gaze flicked in the direction of her backside. "You know. Sorry. But nice. Very nice.''

"That's quite all right," she said, stifling a grin.

"See you tomorrow, signorina. Ciao."

"Ciao."

As soon as Bruno, the disappointed suitor, was out the door, Sarah closed it and threw the bolt. She didn't need any more surprises this afternoon.

Sarah and Leo spent the rest of the afternoon playing. At least, Leo thought they were playing when she gave him a box of crayons and a sketchbook.

There was nothing particularly distressing in his creations. The human figures he composed were fairly typical stick figures, most of them properly centered on the page and in proper proportion to one another.

When she asked him to draw his father, Leo put a smile on the rounded face of the figure, which was a very good sign. When she asked him to draw his great aunt, Honoria, he did his five-year-old best to cloak her in a big purple gown, and he included a bright red smile on her face, too.

As for himself, when she asked him to draw a self-portrait, Leo chose a straight line for his mouth, a fairly neutral expression. Up to this point, other than his reaction to the one doll, Sarah wasn't picking up on any pathology or emotional dysfunction in the child whatsoever. Leo Chiara seemed very well adjusted in spite of the fact that he chose not to speak.

When Nick called from the hospital to report that his aunt was doing well and that he'd be home after he had the results of a few more tests, Sarah asked him if he'd have time for her to ask him some more questions about the boy this evening.

"Plenty of time," he replied.

"Good. And I have a few questions for you about the recent murder, too."

If he read her tone properly, he'd know just how much she resented being kept in the dark about the crime. And for some odd and inexplicable reason, Sarah really wanted Nick Chiara to read her right. It seemed terribly important to her just then.

He sighed softly at his end of the line and then said, "I didn't tell you about the murder, Sarah, because I don't think it has a thing to do with Leo, or with your safety. It was an isolated incident. Nothing more. But I apologize. You should have been told."

He read her just right, Sarah thought, and she found herself smiling into the receiver.

"Apology accepted," she said. "I really would like to know more about the incident."

"I'll tell you everything I know. And tell my son I'll be home soon with hamburgers and French fries for our dinner. That should make him happy."

"Mmm. That makes me happy, too."

"Good. See you soon."

After she hung up the phone, Sarah headed toward Leo's room to give him the good hamburger news. It seemed a shame to be in someplace as exotic as Montebello and still be scarfing down burgers and fries, but maybe tomorrow she and Leo could wander out and find a nice little restaurant.

Just as she was passing through the living room, the front doorbell rang. After Bruno's unanticipated arrival in the kitchen, she didn't know whom to expect as she walked to the door. Maybe she shouldn't even open it, she thought, in light of the murderer still on the loose.

"Who is it?" she called, deciding to play it safe, while her hand was still on the door knob.

"It's the Davis-Finches," came the reply. "Leo's

grandparents. We've come to take him on vacation with us.''

Ah. Another little detail they hadn't told her about. Sarah opened the door.

"Oh, dear," the woman who was obviously Mrs. Davis-Finch exclaimed. "Why, you're not Estella."

"No. I'm Sarah."

"Where's Estella?" Mr. Davis-Finch inquired.

Sarah sighed. "That seems to be the question of the day. Please, come in."

Chapter 8

At seven o'clock that evening, Nick walked along a quiet corridor on the sixth floor of King Augustus Hospital, and then turned into one of the spacious private rooms reserved for the Sebastiani family. There, he discovered his Aunt Honoria sitting up in bed, alert and looking just as healthy as all the tests had indicated.

The EKG. The bloodwork. The X rays. The MRI. He'd done everything but put her on a treadmill. Every test he'd ordered had come back not just within normal ranges, but showing his elderly aunt to be in exceptionally good health for her weight and advanced age.

"How do you feel, love?" he asked, plucking her

chart from the foot of the bed before angling a hip onto the high mattress. "Are you comfortable?"

"Quite," she said, keeping her gaze on the television screen overhead while she punched buttons on a remote device. "There aren't as many channels on this dratted thing as there are on our television set at home."

"Probably not." Nick closed the chart and put it back. "But you won't have to put up with it for very long. I imagine you'll be coming home tomorrow."

"Do you think so, dear?" She continued to glare at the ever changing screen at the foot of the bed.

"All of your tests came back fine, Aunt Honoria. We'll just keep you here this evening for observation. Merely to be cautious. But I honestly don't see any reason at all for you to remain in hospital any longer than that."

"If you say so, Nicky," she murmured.

Nick studied her face, not as her physician now but as her nephew. Honoria Satherwaite seemed oddly calm and content for a woman who'd just been rushed to the emergency room. Other than her disappointment over the number of channels on the television, she didn't seem to have a care in the world, and that casual attitude of hers only served to increase Nick's suspicion that his aunt had faked her fall for some reason he couldn't begin to fathom.

He'd suspected the fraud from the very beginning this afternoon, when he'd discovered her lying in a rather comfortable pose on the living-room floor, with her legs stretched out straight, her arms folded across her midsection, all of her necklaces in order, and her lavender gown smoothed out quite nicely all about her.

An unexpected fall of a woman his aunt's size should have taken out a lamp or two, at the very least, if not a large piece of furniture. Although she claimed to have been dizzy before the fall, her pulse rate had been normal and her pupils both equal and reactive. But he hadn't wanted to take any chances so he'd called for an ambulance and admitted her to the hospital.

Whatever the devil she'd intended to accomplish with her little ruse, other than nearly frightening him to death, he hoped she was satisfied now.

"They should be bringing your dinner shortly," he told her.

"I must say I'm looking forward to it," she said with a slightly sardonic roll of her eyes.

"The food is quite good here, I'm told."

She clucked her tongue. "That remains to be seen, doesn't it? Why don't you run along now, dear? Go home. I'm sure I'm in excellent hands here."

Nick kissed her cheek. "Call me if you need anything. Promise."

"I promise."

"And don't run the nurses ragged."

"No, darling. Of course I won't. Run along now.

Off with you. Hug dear little Leo for me. And give my regards to the lovely Ms. Hunter, will you?''

Half an hour later, juggling a warm sack of burgers and fries in one hand and two bottles of red wine in the other, Nick realized that the lovely Ms. Hunter had bolted the door from the terrace. Afraid of murderers, no doubt. He knocked once on the glass pane, then once again, a little bit louder, before he saw her sprinting through the kitchen toward him.

"I'm glad you're back," she said when she opened the door to let him in. "How's Lady Satherwaite?"

"Better. Fine, actually," he said, stepping into the kitchen. "We don't usually lock this door, Sarah. It really isn't necessary. You needn't be afraid of anyone breaking in."

"Really? Well, then you've probably never met Bruno," she said with a laugh.

"Who?"

"Bruno. Estella's boyfriend. He was the first unexpected visitor this afternoon." She gestured over her shoulder toward the living room. "The second batch is in there."

Nick didn't have a clue what she was talking about. Americans, in his experience, were generally straightforward. They said just what they meant. Sarah Hunter seemed to be speaking in some strange code. He wondered if that was because she was a psychologist.

He put the bag of food and the bottle of wine on the table. "What visitors?" he asked.

"Your in-laws, Sir Dominic. Mr. And Mrs. Davis-Finch. They've come to take Leo on holiday."

"They've what?" He turned toward the door to the living room where he could now clearly hear his mother-in-law's voice. Edith Davis-Finch always trilled like a canary. Good God. "A holiday? I don't know anything about this."

Sarah shrugged. "Apparently they worked out the details with Estella, the former nanny. They've been planning this trip for several months, I gather."

"We'll see about that."

Lara's parents doted on their only grandchild, and traveled from England at least three or four times a year to see him. Nick usually made himself scarce during those visits, because as much as they doted on Leo, the Davis-Finches regarded Leo's father as the incompetent monster who'd let their only daughter die.

They were terrible snobs, neither one of whom had ever thought Sir Dominic Chiara was good enough for Lara Elizabeth Wellington Davis-Finch. Edith, his mother-in-law, had been reasonably civil to Nick over the years. Roger, on the other hand, was barely able to unclench his teeth enough to say a mere hello. After Lara died, both of her parents began to speak to Nick only when absolutely necessary. Aunt Honoria was usually the intermediary.

Still, Edith and Roger Davis-Finch were good to Leo, and in the long run, that was all that really mattered to Nick.

Except for this unanticipated and rather high-handed attempt to spirit his son away to God knows where.

"My son's not going anywhere," he snarled, turning toward the living room.

"Well…"

Sarah put a hand on his arm, restraining him.

"Wait a minute, Nick. It might not be such a bad idea," she said. "I've been thinking about Leo and this trip for the past hour or so, and I think it's a good idea."

Nick turned back to see her intensely serious expression. Gone was the lighthearted look he was accustomed to seeing on Sarah Hunter's pretty face. The playful glitter in her green eyes was gone. The upward tilt of her lips had flattened out to a somber line. She looked serious and utterly professional right now.

"What do you mean?" he asked.

"Leo was absolutely thrilled to see his grandparents this afternoon, Nick. And he's really excited about this trip to Disneyland in Paris. I mean, *really* excited. You should see him. The kid is bouncing around the house like a little rubber ball. A few minutes ago I swear he almost laughed out loud."

"Really?"

She nodded. "Really."

Rather than storm into the other room to confront his in-laws, perhaps even ram his fist into Roger's implacable grimace, Nick slumped into a chair at the kitchen table.

"In other words, you're telling me to let him go," he said. It wasn't a question, but a flat statement.

"That's my professional opinion."

"What about your therapy with him?"

"It will keep," she said. "He'll only be gone for three or four days at the very most. And I honestly believe that getting away from here for a while is the best thing for Leo right now."

"Why?"

Her pretty face turned even more somber and her tone became almost grim. "Because I'm convinced that something happened here, on the palace grounds, something traumatic, that caused your son's silence, and that continues to prevent him from speaking."

A week ago, before all of Leo's tests were complete, Nick might have vehemently disagreed. But without being able to point to a specific physical cause, he couldn't very well refute or even dispute what Sarah was telling him. As a scientist, he hated not having answers. As a father, he felt suddenly helpless and adrift.

Those emotions must have been written across his face, because Sarah reached out and put her hand in his, then squeezed gently.

"I'm going to help him, Nick. I promise you. Please trust me."

At the moment, he didn't see that he had much choice.

Sarah left the kitchen and headed for Leo's room to see if she could be of any help packing. When she'd last been in there, Leo had crammed so many toys in his suitcase that there was no room for his clothes.

His grandmother showed deep affection for and infinite patience with the child, which heartened Sarah and further convinced her that this trip was not only a good idea, but could turn out to be therapeutic for the little boy. And Edith Davis-Finch had been pleasant enough to Sarah in her capacity as nanny without seeming genuinely warm.

"I do believe we're packed," Mrs. Davis-Finch said when Sarah entered the room.

"That's good." Sarah watched Leo stuff just one more teddy bear into the open suitcase.

"I'd like a word with you, Sarah," the woman said quietly. "In private, if you please."

"Sure."

Sarah had been just about to request a word in private herself to give Mrs. Davis-Finch a few suggestions about coping with Leo's silence. Both grandparents seemed distressed about his condition. She didn't want them to push him too hard or actually demand that he speak. The resultant frustration and stress could have devastating long-term effects.

Without disclosing her true identity as a psychologist, Sarah had explained to Mrs. Davis-Finch that there was nothing physically wrong with Leo, that he was getting the very best professional help, and his problem would undoubtedly be cured within a few weeks. The woman seemed rather baffled by it all. Well, Sarah couldn't blame her. She was a bit baffled herself.

She bent now to help the boy jam the poor teddy bear into the suitcase beside his Ernie doll, his soccer ball, and his bright red CD player.

Then, quickly closing and zipping the case before he was inspired to put something else inside it, she said, "Leo, your daddy is in the kitchen. I know you want to give him a great big hug before you go."

He hugged her first, then went dashing down the hall toward the kitchen.

Edith Davis-Finch perched on the edge of Leo's bed. "This is for you, Sarah." She reached out and pressed something into Sarah's hand.

It turned out to be a hundred dollar bill. Sarah blinked down at the round face of Ben Franklin.

"I don't know if your predecessor, Estella, told you about the little arrangement we had with her," the woman said, "but my husband and I would like to continue the arrangement now that you're our grandson's nanny."

"Arrangement?"

"Yes. In return for a gratuity each month…" She gestured toward the bill in Sarah's hand. "Estella was kind enough to keep us informed of our grandson's activities. We're so far away, you know, and we see him so infrequently. The regular news just helps to ease our hearts and minds."

"I'll be happy to do that, Mrs. Davis-Finch," she said, handing the money back. "This isn't necessary. I'm sure Dr. Chiara or Lady Satherwaite would be only too happy to…"

Edith Davis-Finch cut her off. "I'm afraid you don't understand. As concerned grandparents, my husband and I expect to be kept informed about *everything* that goes on here in Leo's house. Not just with the boy. With everything and everyone."

Ah. All of a sudden Sarah got it. Estella had been spying on Nick and his aunt, ratting them out to the in-laws for a hundred bucks a month. Or more. The hundred-dollar bill was probably just the opening bid of Mrs. Davis-Finch's nasty negotiations.

Now, more than ever before, Sarah wanted to get her hands on this Estella chick.

She was tempted to keep the money just to spite Leo's grandmother. But she handed it back with a curt, "Sorry. I don't have time for stuff like that. I'll be happy to send you detailed reports about Leo, though, and lots of pictures."

"We could offer you more," the woman said. "We could make it worth your while."

"No, you couldn't," Sarah said. "Excuse me. I'm going to check on Leo."

She found them in the kitchen—father and son—feeding each other ketchup-drenched French fries.

"I think they're ready to go," she said.

She saw the smile on Nick's handsome face evaporate, and she was aware of the effort he made to get just a portion of it back.

"You're going to have a wonderful time, Leo," he said, picking up his son and hugging him hard. "I wish I could come with you."

The boy's eyes lit up then, so much so that his father immediately knew he had made a mistake.

"I wish I could, but I can't. I'll be far too busy at the hospital. But next summer you and I will go back. Just the two of us."

Leo was nodding enthusiastically when his grandmother appeared in the kitchen doorway.

"We'll be off now, Dominic," she announced coolly.

With his son still in his arms, Nick said, "Hello, Edith. How are you? And Roger?"

"Fine," she answered, her gaze flicking to her watch. "If we don't leave right this minute, I'm afraid we'll miss our flight."

After one final long, hard hug, Nick set his son

down on the ground. "I love you, Leo," he said
softly as the child skipped toward the door.

From his seat on the terrace, Nick kept an eye on
the sunset while he tried to ignore the slamming of
the taxi doors on the other side of the house. Sarah
was right, he told himself. It was good for the boy
to get away for a few days. Leo had always longed
to go to Disneyland. He'd said it often, when he was
speaking. Nick had had every intention of taking
him, but...

He watched Sarah walk around the side of the
house, her gaze riveted on the sunset, a nostalgic
smile clinging to her lips.

"They're gone, I take it," he said.

"Oh. I didn't see you there. Yes, they're gone."
As she passed behind his chair, her fingers lightly
touched his shoulder. "He'll be fine, Nick. He was
so excited."

She was all slim grace and long legs as she slipped
into the chair next to his. Nick leaned forward for
the bottle of wine he'd brought outside. He picked
up the extra empty glass, splashed some of the burgundy into it, and handed it to Sarah.

"Thanks," she said.

"To Leo," he said, raising his own glass.

"And to Mickey Mouse," she added with a little
laugh. "Do you know that I grew up in California

and I've never once been to Disneyland? Isn't that sad? How could I have been so deprived?''

''I can't imagine. Even I've been there.''

''Really? When?''

''When I was in medical school in the States. I went to the one in Orlando, Florida on spring break. I can't claim to remember more than a few hours of the trip, though. Most of it was seen through an alcoholic haze, I'm afraid.''

She laughed again. ''How utterly American. No wonder you speak English so well.''

''I have my aunt to thank for that.''

''Oh, that's right. I forgot. How is she, by the way?''

''Fine,'' he said, taking another sip of his wine. ''I'm ninety-nine percent convinced the old girl's faking.''

''Faking!'' Her eyes widened considerably. ''Why in the world would she do that?''

Nick leaned forward for the wine bottle and splashed a little more of the dark burgundy into his glass. ''I have a theory, if you'd like to hear it.''

''Absolutely.''

''I think my aunt wanted the two of us to be alone. As a matter of fact, I wouldn't be at all surprised if she'd known about the Davis-Finches and their Disneyland excursion all along, and somehow conveniently forgot to mention it to me.''

"Why?" Sarah asked again, eyes still impossibly wide, unimaginably green.

Her face was tinted rose in the reflected light of the sunset. There were golden highlights in her hair. The woman was absolutely lovely. Unless the wine was having a greater effect on him than he imagined, Nick thought he'd never seen a woman quite so beautiful.

Why indeed would his Aunt Honoria, the clever and relentless but heretofore unsuccessful match-maker, seek to strand the two of them together? After more than four years of finding fault with nearly every eligible female in the kingdom of Montebello, had Lady Honoria Delphinia Satherwaite finally deemed the imported Sarah Hunter worthy of her precious nephew?

He shook his head. "I don't have a clue," he murmured, suddenly a bit overwhelmed by the prospect of courting a woman again after all this time. He'd been married for two years, widowed and celibate for another four and a half. To say he was out of practice was an understatement. To say he was afraid was probably closer to the truth. Scared to death, in fact.

He would have laughed if he hadn't felt like such an inept fool. Instead, he drained the wine that remained in his glass and reached for the bottle again.

"Why don't I go in and warm up those hamburgers for us?" Sarah suggested.

"Good idea," he replied.

* * *

In the kitchen, while she counted along with the final seconds of the microwave timer, Sarah stared out the door that led to the terrace.

Two days ago, if anybody had told her she'd be watching the sun as it dipped into the darkening Mediterranean tonight, she would have laughed in that person's face. If anybody had told her that the same ravishing pink, gold and orange sunset would also be framing the most glorious man she'd ever seen in her life—a man called Sir Dominic—a knight, yet!—she would have laughed just before she said "Get outta here."

But there he sat in all his sunset-colored glory, left ankle resting on right knee, dark head tipped back, dark eyes closed, a wineglass dangling from his relaxed hand. What a picture. It belonged in *Esquire* or *GQ*.

She was glad when the microwave dinged and called her attention back to burgers and the real world, where she suddenly found herself as a psychologist without a patient. It wasn't that she couldn't use the extra time to do some additional research on mutism in children, but then she couldn't very well sit with her nose in a book or journal for twelve or fourteen hours a day. Not in fairy-tale Montebello, anyway.

As she arranged the piping hot burgers on the

plates, Sarah decided that she'd rent a car and do some leisurely exploring of the beautiful island kingdom. If only Warren were here to…

Warren!

Good Lord. She'd meant to call him earlier today, but with all the unexpected visitors, it had completely slipped her mind. What time was it in San Francisco now?

Sarah glanced at the clock on the microwave. Okay. It was almost seven o'clock here, so that would make it… Oh, hell. What would that make it back home? Three or four in the morning was the best that she could figure. If she called her fiancé at three or four in the morning, he was liable to have a heart attack before he ever got to the phone. She'd called him once a little before midnight and frightened him so badly he'd hyperventilated for fifteen minutes.

Or was it three or four in the afternoon? How could she be as intelligent as she was and not be able to get a handle on this time zone difference?

She decided not to call. Presumably her father had relayed her whereabouts to Warren. If not, then it wouldn't take him more than one or two phone calls to find out.

It was getting dark, so before she carried their plates outside, Sarah hit the switch for the terrace lights. The palm trees lit up and the pink blossoms on the azaleas were evident again. She kept forgetting she was in paradise.

"What a gorgeous night," she said, setting the plates on the glass-topped table and then sliding into a chair.

"Tomorrow should be even better," Nick said. "What would you like to do?"

"Do?" She had just taken a bite of her burger so the word came out muffled. More like *Dpf.*

"Well, I was sitting here thinking while you were in the kitchen, and it occurred to me that we're both out of jobs for the next few days. We might as well make the best of it."

"You don't have to entertain me, Nick. Honest. I have plenty of psych journals to keep me busy, and I thought maybe I'd rent a car and tool around the island a little. Maybe find a quiet beach, or something."

"I know just the place," he said.

"Oh, good. Where?"

His eyes glittered merrily. "It's in a very secluded spot. I'll have to show you."

Sarah was about to demur, but then a wicked thought darted through her brain. She wondered what Sir Dominic, the pirate's progeny, looked like in a pair of swimming trunks.

After all, she was a scientist, wasn't she? And any scientist worth her salt pursued her curiosity until she was thoroughly satisfied with the answer. Sarah couldn't imagine being anything but thoroughly satisfied with the answer to this question.

Even so, she shouldn't.

Should she?

Probably not.

Definitely not.

"I'd love to," she said even before she realized that her mouth was open.

Chapter 9

The next morning, on their way to the Lido—which was Montebello's fancy name for the kingdom's finest white sand beach—Sarah and Nick stopped by the hospital to check on Lady Satherwaite.

As the daughter and sister of physicians, it came as no surprise to Sarah that the moment they walked through the front door of the hospital, half a dozen people were vying for Dr. Chiara's attention. The husband of a patient collared him, wanting to know when his wife could leave the hospital. A nervous and very apologetic young man in scrubs needed some quick advice. A young candy striper with big gooey eyes apparently required her hunk fix for the day, and what better way to get it than accosting

Doctor Hunk himself. An elderly woman in a robe and slippers offered Nick a rose.

After standing by patiently for fifteen minutes, Sarah finally excused herself.

"I'll meet you in your aunt's room," she said, and hopped into an elevator to the private sixth floor, where she had to pass through yet another metal detector and identification grilling before being allowed entrance to the royal wing.

She didn't really mind preceding Nick in order to have a few minutes alone with Lady Satherwaite because she wanted to ask a few questions about the former nanny, Estella. When she entered the room, which was more like a posh hotel suite than any hospital room that Sarah had ever seen, Nick's aunt was just finishing her breakfast.

"Come in, Sarah, dear. How lovely to see you this morning. Would you care for a cup of coffee? An English muffin?"

"No, thanks." Sarah took the breakfast tray and put it on a table before she perched on the foot of the bed. "You're looking well rested this morning."

"Ha! No thanks to the nurses and interns who insisted on prodding and poking at me all night long." The big woman gave a snort. "I don't know how they expect anyone to get any rest at all in this place. It was like Paddington Station. No sooner had one person left than another took his place."

Sarah chuckled softly, then she leaned forward and

raised a suspicious eyebrow. "Rumor has it, Lady Satherwaite, that you're malingering."

"I?" The woman's hand, minus rings and bracelets now, jerked upward and splayed out over her gigantic bosom. "Malingering? Who dared to say that? What wicked beast would ever accuse me of such a thing?"

"Your nephew," Sarah said.

"Really."

"Uh-huh."

Honoria Satherwaite's mouth twitched in a grin. "And does my wicked beast of a nephew have any sort of theory as to why I might want to malinger here?"

"Yes. As a matter of fact, he does." Sarah bit down on a grin of her own.

"And that theory would be…?"

"To ensure that we would find ourselves alone. I think he smells a bit of matchmaking."

"Why! The very idea."

"I told Nick he must be wrong," Sarah said with her tongue firmly planted in her cheek. "I told him you'd never do anything so underhanded."

"Quite right, my dear." Her grin widened. She winked one pale blue eye. "Is my little scheme working?"

Sarah laughed out loud. "No. And it isn't going to, either."

Lady Satherwaite's smile turned upside down and

the creases in her forehead suddenly multiplied. "Oh, dear. Is there someone else? Someone back home in California? I must admit that possibility never entered my mind. Although I don't know why it wouldn't have, a young woman as attractive as you. Is it too late for Nicky? Are you already spoken for? Are you already wildly in love with someone else, Sarah, dear?"

For a moment Sarah didn't know what to say. It was true that she was spoken for, but as for being wildly in love with someone, namely Warren Dill… Well, no, that wasn't the case. Still, that didn't mean that she wasn't engaged to be married. She doubted if Lady Satherwaite, the obvious romantic, would understand the situation. After all, hardly anybody did.

"No, I'm not wildly in love," she replied, leaving it at that before changing the subject. "Do you feel well enough this morning for me to ask you a couple of questions about Estella, Leo's former nanny? I won't if you're not up to it."

"I'm well enough to know when I'm being distracted," she said with a laugh. "What do you want to know about Estella? She wasn't a particularly interesting young woman, although she did strike me as fairly competent. And Leo seemed to enjoy her well enough. At least he didn't dislike her. Nicky let her go because he wanted more private time with Leo."

"Actually, I'd like her name and address so that I

can speak with her myself. I hope to find out a little more about the night of the fire.'' She narrowed her gaze as she added, ''And the murder, which no one bothered to tell me about.''

''Pish.'' Lady Satherwaite clucked her tongue. ''No one wanted to worry you unnecessarily. It has nothing to do with poor Leo, I'm quite certain.''

''Nevertheless, I'd still like to ask Estella a few questions. May I have her address?''

''Bring me my handbag. They stashed it in a drawer somewhere over there.''

While Sarah was opening and closing drawers, she heard Lady Satherwaite exclaim, ''There you are, my darling!''

Sarah looked in the mirror to find Nick framed in the doorway. What was wrong with her, that her heart kept slamming against her ribs at the mere sight of this man?

''Sorry I'm late,'' he said. ''I should have known that the minute I walked into the building somebody would find something for me to do. How are you this morning, Aunt Honoria?''

''Still a bit dizzy when I get up, but I don't expect you to believe me, dear. At any rate, I've told the nurses that I'll be staying at least a few more days.''

''So they tell me,'' he murmured. ''I hope you don't mind that Sarah and I have made plans in your absence.''

''Mind? Of course, I don't mind.'' She clapped

her hands. "I think it's delightful. Tell me. What do you plan to do?"

Just then, Sarah discovered Lady Satherwaite's handbag in the bottom right drawer of the bureau.

"Ah-ha! Before we do anything, we're going to talk to Estella," she said, "if you'll give us her address."

She handed the bag to Nick's aunt, who opened it and pulled out a small black address book. "I'm sure it's in here. Her last name is Verdi, as I recall. Under *V*. Or I might have written it under *N* for nanny. Here, dear. Take the whole book. I have absolutely no need for it at the moment."

"Thank you." Sarah tucked the little book in the pocket of her jacket. "I'll take good care of it."

"Doesn't matter." She lifted her huge shoulders in a shrug. "If anyone in there wants me, they know where they can find me. Now, if you don't mind, I believe I'll take a little nap. Nicky, will you please tell the nurses not to disturb me?"

"I don't have much clout with the nurses, love, but I'll do my best." He leaned down to kiss his aunt's forehead. "See you this evening. Behave yourself."

"Have a good time, you two," she said, closing her eyes. "Don't rush back on my account. Enjoy."

Fifteen minutes later, as Nick was pulling out of the hospital parking lot, he glanced over at Sarah in the passenger seat. Her head was bent forward as she flipped pages and concentrated on notations in the little address book. If she thought his aunt was half-demented and wholly eccentric, she hadn't said so. In fact, she seemed quite happy to comply with the old girl's bizarre, romantic demands.

Enjoy.

He wasn't sure he knew how to do that anymore. Enjoy himself. He wasn't sure he wanted to enjoy himself, or to start something he had no intention of finishing. Actually, at the moment, he wasn't sure of anything but the way Sarah's hair was streaked with gold in the sunlight and the flowery fragrance—was it gardenias?—coming from her direction, and the fact that his temperature seemed to spike whenever he was in her presence.

"Ah-ha!" she said. "I think I found it. Estella Verdi. Here she is, listed under *C* of all things."

Nick laughed. "That would be *C* for composer. Knowing my aunt, it makes perfect sense."

"She lives at 5143B Avenue Royale. Do you know where that is?"

"I can find it," he said, changing lanes in order to head toward the north side of San Sebastian. The older part of the city. "Tell me once again just what it is you hope to find out from her."

"More about the fire and the murder, and how they might be connected to Leo's silence."

"Leo was completely unaware of them, Sarah. I

asked the nanny. More than once, believe me. Estella assured me that he slept through the entire series of events that night.''

"So you say," she murmured. "I don't suppose Estella told you anything about Bruno, did she?''

"Who the hell is Bruno?''

"Estella's fiancé. Or at least he would be her fiancé if he knew where she lived. I'm not a detective, but that leads me to believe that the time the two of them spent together must've been at your house rather than hers.''

Nick took his eyes off the road just long enough to see the intense expression on her face. Her green eyes were brilliant as emeralds. Her mouth was set in a firm and stubborn line. There was no doubt she was serious about this.

"How do you know all this?'' he asked. "You've only been here a few days.''

"I'm a good listener. That's my job. And since in this case, I can't very well listen to my patient, I have to listen to everyone who's been around him lately.''

He kept forgetting that she wasn't just the lovely new nanny, but a psychologist, and presumably an excellent one, sent for by King Marcus. What else didn't he know about her, he wondered. How old was she? Why wasn't she married? Why did his looney aunt seem to believe they would be good together? Would they? Did he even want to find out?

The streets were narrow and the corners treacherous in the old part of town.

"How long have you been a psychologist?" he asked as he peered at the street numbers along Avenue Royale.

On the other side of the car, she was silent a long moment before crossing her arms and leaning her back against the door. Out of the corner of his eye, Nick could see the challenging expression on her face. Still, there was a touch of playfulness in her tone when she said, "What? All of a sudden you're interested in my credentials, Dr. Chiara?"

He pulled the car next to the curb on the right and killed the engine. "No, *Ms.* Hunter. All of a sudden I'm interested in *you.*"

"Oh." She made a tiny gulping sound, then asked, "Why are you stopping?"

"We're here." He nodded toward the stucco apartment building up ahead. "Casa Estella."

The ancient four-story building was dark inside. Its hallways smelled of garlic and olive oil and decades of cooked fish. Estella, naturally, lived on the top floor. Nick stood back while Sarah knocked on the door.

The nanny wasn't thrilled to see them. Sarah knew that as soon as the young woman opened the door and blinked the moment she realized that her former employer had come calling. The color drained from

Estella's olive complexion and her gaze kept darting from Nick to Sarah to the floor and who knows where. The girl made eye contact about as well as a jellyfish, and all of a sudden she could barely speak Italian, much less English.

After Estella stood in the doorway, reciting the same old story about Leo sleeping through the night when the murder and fire took place, Sarah was utterly convinced the girl was lying, but still she pressed her for more.

"It's very important that we know the truth about that night, Estella," she urged. "Please won't you help us?"

Nick translated, just to be sure the girl understood.

"Si. Si. I know. It's true what I tell you. I swear," she wailed. "I did a good job, Sir Dominic. I did nothing wrong. I felt much affection for Leo."

While she was protesting, from behind her in the apartment, a gruff male voice called out her name, and the girl looked more panicky than ever.

"Si, Papa," she answered over her shoulder, before telling Sarah, "That is all I know. I must ask you to go now. I am sorry."

Sarah wasn't budging.

"Tell us about Bruno, Estella," she demanded.

The nanny's eyes practically pinwheeled now. "I know nothing. You must go now. Ciao. Goodbye."

She slammed the door.

Sarah was tempted to kick it in, but Nick drew her

away with a firm hand on her arm and led her toward the stairs.

"She's lying through her teeth, Nick," Sarah muttered through her own clenched teeth. "Can't you tell?"

"Yes. I can tell. And I can also tell that young Estella probably lives with an overprotective and very strict father who would quite happily blow you away with his shotgun when you barged into his residence uninvited."

"Oh," she answered, starting down the stairs.

"This isn't America, you know."

"No, I guess not." She sighed. "Well, what are we going to do? Whatever it is she knows, I need to know in order to help your son. I'm certain of that now more than ever."

"We'll figure something out. Perhaps we could have her come back to the house to pick up something she left behind. Or a final paycheck. Or something. That way she could speak without her father overhearing. We'll figure it out while we're lying on the beach."

"I'm really not in the mood anymore."

Sarah realized she sounded petulant, maybe even sullen, but she just couldn't help it. She didn't like people getting in her way, coming between her and what she needed to know about her patients. She didn't like wasting time, especially now, when she had so little to begin with.

It wasn't just that she was feeling thwarted, either. She was beginning to question Nick's sincerity in wanting to help her. She wanted Nick to be a bit more eager, if not relentless, in pursuit of the causes of his son's silence.

Maybe the man didn't care, after all. Maybe, because he was a physician and this wasn't a physical problem, he didn't believe the boy could be helped. Maybe…

They had reached the bottom of the stairs now, but instead of continuing toward the door, Nick stopped. He put a hand on each of her shoulders, turned her toward him, then tipped her chin up with a finger.

The dark foyer was lit only by streaks of sunlight coming through a narrow, grimy windowpane. But each of those streaks of light glistened in his dark eyes as he gazed down at her.

"My son means everything to me," he said softly. "Don't ever be confused about that, Sarah. All right? Not for a second. Leo is my life."

"I'm glad," she whispered.

A corner of his mouth quirked up. "But that doesn't mean I can't take you to the beach."

"That's true, but…"

"And while we're lying on the beach," he continued, "I want you to tell me everything you know about mutism, as well as everything you don't know, but want an answer for. I want you to educate me,

Sarah, so I can help my son just as much as you. Will you do that? Please?''

For a moment she thought he was going to kiss her, the way he continued to stare into her eyes, the way his thumb began to stroke her jaw. It would have been wonderful. It would have been heart-stopping. Soul-scorching.

It would have been completely unprofessional, she told herself as she stepped back.

''Yes,'' she said. ''I'll do my best. I'll be happy to try.''

As far as classrooms went, the Lido below the high cliffs of San Sebastian held more than a few distractions. With its endless stretch of white sand, it rivaled any beach that Sarah had ever seen in her home state of California and was lovelier than the *playa* where she had spent so much time during her Peace Corps stint in El Salvador.

There were seagulls strung out in groups at the edge of the water, and terns doing cartwheels in the high breezes overhead. The September sun was like melted butter.

And Nick Chiara looked better in a swimsuit than any human being had a right to.

Sarah rolled over on her side, just to take another peek while his eyes were closed, as they had been for the past few minutes. It seemed as if the warmth of the sun and the beach sounds were lulling both of them to sleep.

She peeked. Just a little. It wasn't easy not reaching out to trace a finger along the sleek, suntan lotion-slicked curve of his upper arm or to test the softness of the dark hair on his chest. Her gaze followed the dark, damp line that disappeared beneath the waistband of his black trunks. Oh brother. This probably hadn't been such a good idea after all.

The plan had been to use the time that Leo was away to read through the huge stack of journals she'd brought with her, to further educate herself about the boy's condition, instead of lazing on a beach, blabbing everything she already knew and quickly approaching the limits of her expertise.

Nick Chiara was as smart as he was gorgeous. He was a perfect student, asking intelligent and pointed questions, ones that made Sarah dig deeper into her own reservoir of knowledge about child psychology and human behavior to come up with equally intelligent answers. And miracle of miracles, he even seemed interested in all she had to say. Most people, even Warren, tended to doze off if she got started discussing a case, while Nick seemed to hang on her every word.

Well…until both of them succumbed to the slumberous effects of the Mediterranean sun and the lullaby of the seagulls and the lapping tide.

She sighed, thinking she could stay here forever,

listening to the sea, looking from beneath her lashes at this perfectly sculpted person who...

...opened his eyes and smiled at her just then.

"I thought you were sleeping," he said.

She shook her head.

"Tired?" he asked.

Again, she shook her head.

"Tell me more, then. Teach me."

Sarah didn't need to be asked twice.

"All right. There's another theory about mutism that I haven't told you about yet. This is from a team of clinicians in Alabama, as I recall, who maintain that the self-imposed silence is merely an attention-getting tactic. According to them, a child who refuses to speak suddenly thrusts himself into the center of the family universe, even more than the child who screams and acts out."

"Makes sense," Nick murmured.

"I suppose. To a certain extent. I don't see that it applies at all in Leo's case, though. First of all because he's an only child. The Alabama study focused on children with two or more siblings. Second, because it's obvious that you and Lady Satherwaite absolutely dote on him. Leo couldn't be any more central to your family universe if he were the sun itself." She squinted as she pointed upward toward the real thing blazing overhead.

Nick turned on his side and levered up on an elbow. "Which brings us back to your trauma theory, right?"

"Right." Sarah had to remind herself to maintain eye contact. Her gaze kept longing to drift toward his chest. How unprofessional was that, for heaven's sake?

"And there's no helping Leo unless we identify the significant event or events?"

"I wouldn't say there's no helping him," she said. "Only that we'd be on firmer ground if we knew what happened to make him stop speaking. Knowing is always better than guessing, even though we're forced to do plenty of that in my business."

He flopped over on his stomach now, so Sarah no longer had to worry about being distracted by his chest. Now she was looking at the smooth, glistening curve of his back.

"We do that in my business, too, I'm afraid," he said.

Sarah laughed. "Not that many of you admit it." A physician who didn't think of himself as God or the next best thing to Him, she marveled. Would wonders never cease? "I'm pretty sure my father would rather stand before a firing squad than admit that medicine is an art as well as a science."

"I heard your father lecture five or six years ago at a conference in Helsinki. He knows his stuff."

"That he does," she said with a sigh.

"Your brother followed in his footsteps, didn't he?"

"Uh-huh."

Those dark eyes zeroed in on hers. "So why didn't you, little Sarah?" he asked softly.

She was about to give him her stock reply—"I kept flunking chemistry"—accompanied with the usual carefree laugh and a breezy wave of her hand, when suddenly she wanted nothing more than to tell him the truth, to reveal her true self to this man.

This wasn't supposed to happen. It was normally Sarah, psychologist extraordinaire, who delved into others' minds and hearts, who dredged up secrets from their souls while she maintained a cool and pleasant distance. It wasn't supposed to be the other way around.

She tried to identify all the emotions whizzing through her, nearly making her dizzy, and not only was she unable to identify them, but she couldn't even tell if they were positive or negative. Everything seemed topsy-turvy all of a sudden.

"Why didn't you?" Nick asked again.

His mouth was a patient curve. Sarah noticed the tiny crow's feet at the corners of his eyes, the shadow along his jawline, the beguiling little dent centered in his chin. What had he asked her? All she could think of just then was that she'd never wanted to be kissed so much in her life.

When she finally opened her mouth to speak, she

wasn't entirely sure what words were going to come spilling out.

"We should probably go," she said. "I'm... It's really getting hot."

Chapter 10

It wasn't at all like Sarah to avoid a problem or to postpone a confrontation, but that's exactly what she did for the next six hours. Avoidance became her middle name. Mañana was good enough for her. The day after mañana might be even better.

Her problem was this damned visceral reaction she kept having toward Nick Chiara. Falling into the dark depths of his eyes. Getting goose bumps at the sound of his voice. Being entranced by the curve of his back and the texture of his skin. She barely knew the man, but suddenly her internal temperature was intimately related to whether or not he was within a few feet of her.

It reminded her of the way she'd felt about Billy

Dean when she was in grade school. It was just ridiculous.

The moment she returned from the Lido—while
Nick headed back to the hospital to see his aunt—
Sarah picked up the phone and made her long over-
due call to Warren, hoping that the sound of her
fiancé's no-nonsense, brass-tacks-and-paper-clips
voice would bring her back to reality. It was four
o'clock in the afternoon in Montebello, and she had
no idea what time it would be in San Francisco, but
she really didn't care. She needed a strong, sober
dose of Warren Dill, and she needed it *now*.

She called Warren's home number first, and
waited sixteen rings before he answered. The sound
of his sleep-roughened voice made her smile.

"Hi, sleepyhead. It's me," she said, imagining his
rumpled hair, the soft, pale blue pajamas he always
wore that perfectly matched the color of his eyes, the
way he'd be reaching for his glasses right about now,
and then angling the clock radio beside the bed to
get a better view of its red digital readout.

"It's six-oh-nine in the morning, Sarah. For God's
sake."

What a comfort that he knew the exact time. He
was so utterly dependable.

"Well, I'm happy to hear you, too, sweetheart,"
she answered with a laugh.

What a grouch. He always was unless he got
precisely eight hours of sleep. Seven hours wasn't

enough. Nine was too much. It had to be eight hours, plus or minus five minutes. Nothing else would do. She used to think that was cute.

"Where are you?" he asked casually, as if the answer didn't matter one way or another. "I've been trying to call you for the past three days, and nobody in your family or at the clinic seems to have any notion where you are."

Obviously her father hadn't passed along her message on the day she left California, and no one at the clinic was being forthcoming. That didn't surprise Sarah all that much. Warren had a way of asking questions that made peoples' hackles rise. What did surprise her, though, was that Warren didn't sound at all relieved to hear her voice after not knowing where she was all this while.

"You shouldn't have worried about me," she said.

"I wasn't worried, Sarah. Don't be so dramatic. I just couldn't locate you." He sounded so calm and unconcerned. He sounded…well…just like Warren Dill.

"And that didn't worry you?" she asked.

"No. Of course not. Why would it?"

It seemed like such a logical question, but all of a sudden Sarah wasn't feeling logical. Usually she adored Warren's calm disposition and cool logic and total lack of passion. That was one of the reasons she was going to marry him, for heaven's sake. Those were the qualities she wanted in a mate.

Except not right this minute. Right this minute she wanted somebody who really cared about her. Somebody who went overboard. Beyond the pale. Crazy.

"Well, why the hell didn't you worry, Warren?" she snapped. "What if I'd been dead in a ditch somewhere? Or kidnapped? Or wandering around Chinatown with amnesia?"

Her fiancé snorted. "Don't be silly, Sarah."

She wasn't. She was being deadly serious even as she was being melodramatic. How dare he not worry about her? How dare he not track down her father, grab him by the lapels or put a pistol to his head, demanding to know his daughter's whereabouts?

"Sarah? Have you been drinking?" he asked now. "You know how you get."

Yes. She got all warm and comfy with glass or two of red wine. She got irrepressibly sexy with just one sip of champagne. She got horny as hell after two margaritas. That's how she got.

"Sarah?"

"I can't talk right now, Warren. I'm too angry."

"All right." He sighed. The soul of indulgence. The patience of Job. The passion of a "Call me back when you calm down. But, please, not before seven in the morning. Goodbye, sweetheart."

He hung up.

Just like that.

And Sarah sat listening to the dial tone for what seemed like half an hour. It was stupid, she thought, to feel so lost when she knew exactly where she was. It didn't make any sense...to be suddenly angry at Warren for the very qualities she prized in him, and at the same time drawn to Nick by the qualities which she disdained.

"Sarah?"

Nick rapped gently on her bedroom door.

"Sarah?" he said again, a little bit louder.

"Yes?" Her voice sounded farther away than merely the other side of the door.

"I'm back from the hospital. I just wanted to let you know."

"Thanks."

He waited a moment, thinking she might say something else, before he asked, "Shall I take you out for dinner? There's a wonderful café not too far from the palace, and we could..."

"No. Thanks anyway, Nick. I'm just going to read for a while and then I'll probably fall asleep."

Frowning, he looked at his watch. Fall asleep? It wasn't even six o'clock yet.

"Are you all right?" he asked.

"Fine. Just a little tired. Too much sun, probably."

"Anything I can do for you? Would you like me to—"

She cut him off with a "No, thanks. I'll be fine. See you in the morning."

"All right, then. Good night." He stepped away from the door, but turned back. "I'll be close by if you need anything."

"I'm fine. Good night, Nick. Sleep well."

Right.

He just might.

After a cold shower. After half a bottle of cognac.

For an instant, he was tempted to kick in her door like some barbarian, the way his father might have done. To sweep Miss Sarah Hunter up in his arms. To tell her he hadn't felt this way in years. If ever. To tell her…

What?

To tell her that despite his bone-deep worry about his son, he'd still been able to have salacious thoughts about the boy's therapist? To confide that his back was sunburned because he'd had to spend far too much time lying on his stomach at the Lido this afternoon, to avoid exposing his obvious need? Or to confess that a randy teenager was better able to control his ardor, for God's sake?

The trouble was, Nick decided, he'd allowed his aunt's romantic notions to invade his brain. He'd gone five years without a woman, and he'd had every intention of going another forty or fifty years in the same unfettered fashion.

He had his work. His Aunt Honoria was the only woman he really wanted or needed in his life. Most of all, he had Leo.

And suddenly, missing his son incredibly, Nick reached for his wallet and the number that his in-laws had left in case of an emergency. As far as he was concerned, this *was* an emergency of the highest order.

He carried the phone out to the terrace and punched in the endless series of numbers, beginning with the country code for France, hoping the hotel operator spoke English because he wasn't in the mood to use his less-than-fluent French. At last, and in English, the operator connected him to the Davis-Finchs' suite, and it wasn't until his mother-in-law, Edith, picked up the phone that he realized the utter futility of the call.

His son couldn't speak.

Ah, God.

"Edith, it's Nick. I was just calling to check on Leo."

He could actually hear the frost suddenly chilling the edges of her voice when she responded, "He's wonderful. Such a sweet boy. We're all having a lovely time."

Nick waited a moment, hoping she would expand with a few more details about their day at Disney-land, but she didn't. Her breathing sounded increasingly impatient, even perturbed.

"Good," he said. "Well, I'm glad to hear that. I'd like to say hello to him, Edith."

There followed a brief but stony silence. "He's

sleeping right now, Nick. He's had a long day, bless his heart. Perhaps you could call back tomorrow?''

He's my son, goddammit, Nick wanted to shout. And his mother would still be alive if she'd been honest with me about her condition. I could have saved her. I could have saved them both. Damn her, and damn you for thinking otherwise.

"All right. I'll do that. I'll call tomorrow. Has Leo spoken at all while he's been with you and Roger?''

''No,'' she said, icily, the implication being that Leo's silence was as much Nick's fault as Lara's death.

"Tell him I love him, will you, please, Edith?''

"Naturally,'' she snapped. "Goodbye, Nick. It was good of you to call.''

After she broke the connection, he sat listening to the empty space between San Sebastian and Paris. Leo seemed so terribly far away.

It wasn't the first time he'd been separated from his son. He'd had to be away from home numerous times during the past five years for seminars and medical conferences. Why did it bother him so much this time?

Nick shut off the phone. Well, he had a choice, didn't he? He could sit out here and glower at the sunset, feeling morose and sorry for himself, or he could go inside and pour himself three fingers of something one hundred proof, then sit inside and glower at the furniture while feeling morose and sorry for himself.

Self-pity was always better accompanied by a snifter of cognac, so he decided to go inside.

Avoiding her problems was one thing, but by nine o'clock that evening Sarah wasn't able to avoid the relentless growling of her stomach. She closed the psychiatric journal she was reading, slipped on her robe, then stood at her bedroom door, listening—for what, she wasn't sure. Footsteps. Signs of life. *Him.* When the coast sounded clear, she tiptoed into the kitchen.

She flipped on the overhead lights just in time to see Nick Chiara with a brandy snifter in one hand and an egg in the other. Apparently he'd just cracked the egg on the rim of a mixing bowl, but when the sudden lights surprised him, the egg oozed out onto the counter rather than into the waiting bowl, and Nick was left with two halves of an empty eggshell in his hand and a look of disbelief on his face.

For a second, elegant Sir Dominic looked so gorgeously flummoxed, so completely adorable, that Sarah couldn't help but laugh even as she apologized.

"Sorry for startling you. I didn't know you were in here. Let me wipe that up."

She snapped a paper towel off a roll and began to

sop up the yellow mess while Nick stepped aside and dropped the broken eggshell into the trashcan.

"Ah, well. I really didn't need that third egg, anyway," he said, his voice just a bit on the slurry side. "Too much cholesterol."

Too much something, Sarah thought. She peered at the snifter and wondered just how much brandy he had drunk. Enough, obviously. If she had an ounce of brains in her head, she'd turn around and go back to her room posthaste, hungry or not. In her experience, a gorgeous guy on a full tank of brandy wasn't the most trustworthy creature in the world.

But like an idiot, instead of exiting stage left, she heard herself saying, "I make a pretty mean omelet. Why don't you let me take over here?"

"Spoken like a true heroine," he said, lifting his glass in her direction, grinning over the rim, swaying a few degrees from east to west. "What can I do to help?"

"Sit," she said, hoping he'd do precisely that before he keeled over. "Chat me up while I chop. What do you like in your omelet? Onions? Peppers? Cheese?"

"Anything." He sighed almost gratefully as he took a seat at the table, twirled his snifter a moment, then said, "Hundred-year-old brandy has a way of sneaking up on a person."

"I can see that." Sarah spoke as she rummaged

through the refrigerator for more eggs and accompaniments.

"I'm glad you're here, Sarah."

"Hmm," she murmured, pulling a green pepper and a few limp scallions from the vegetable bin. "I'm glad to be here, too."

"No. I mean I'm really glad you're here. You know. Not here as in the kitchen, although God knows I'm glad enough for that. But here in Montebello. What I mean is, I'm glad we've met, even if it is under such damned sorry circumstances." He chuckled deep in his throat. "I'm glad you're beautiful and shapely and smart, instead of some hatchet-faced, wild-eyed psychobabbler who..."

Sarah turned. He was several more sheets to the wind than she'd imagined. "Hatchet-faced, wild-eyed psychobabbler?"

He nodded, apparently quite pleased with himself and his choice of words. His smile slid a little more to the left.

"You're not on call tonight, are you, Dr. Chiara?" she asked, praying that he wasn't, but wondering if she should get a pot of strong coffee brewing just in case.

He shook his head. "No. Not on call. I'm on extended leave, actually. On holiday."

"That's good," she said, breathing a small sigh of relief as she closed the refrigerator door, dumped her stash of vegetables onto the counter, and pushed up the sleeves of her robe. "Well, okay then. One major omelet, coming up."

While Sarah began to chop a fat green pepper, she could feel Nick's dark gaze on her back, or wherever he was looking—probably lower—while he sat behind her. "So, tell me," she said over her shoulder, "when was your last encounter with a hatchet-faced, wild-eyed psychobabbler?"

"I wasn't casting aspersions on your profession," he said. "I meant it as a compliment."

"A compliment." Sarah rolled her eyes. "Oh, I get it. The same sort of compliment as if I said I was glad you aren't some arrogant, concrete-jawed quack."

When he failed to respond, Sarah looked over her shoulder, wondering if she'd gone too far with her comment and made him angry. Doctors, as she well knew, often considered arrogance one of their most valuable qualities and she didn't know anybody who liked being called a quack. If Nick Chiara was angry, though, his grin certainly concealed his temper.

"Yes," he said. "That was what I meant." His brow furrowed. "More or less."

"Well, then, you probably shouldn't compliment me anymore," she told him.

"No. I won't. At least not while you're holding a knife."

Now it was Sarah who grinned. "Good thinking.

You're a lot smarter than I imagined, Dr. Chiara,'' she said.

"So are you, Ms. Hunter. So are you."

He pushed back his chair, grasped the edge of the table to steady himself, and then stood. "And in light of your intelligence, I'm going to go take a good, long, cold, and very sobering shower. You deserve better than to spend the evening with someone who's having a difficult time focusing on you." He chuckled again. "Both of you."

He winked then. Well, it wasn't a wink exactly. It was more of a slow and sexy descent of his right eyelid and thick lashes, enough to cause Sarah's heart to slide south a rib or two.

"I'll be right back."

"Take your time."

Sarah returned her attention to the green pepper she'd been in the process of cutting up. Take a couple hours. Take all night. With any luck, Nick would pass out somewhere between here and the shower.

And with a little bit more luck, she wouldn't chop off a fingertip or two while she waited, stupidly hoping for him to return.

This was a first, she had to admit. A pleasantly pickled man volunteering to sober up in order to be better company for a woman. Pleasantly or not-so-pleasantly pickled men, in her experience, were more likely to suggest that a woman join their boozy state, a preamble to joining them in bed.

Bed. Hmm. She wondered…

Whoa.

Where did that come from?

She was going to lose a whole lot more than a finger if she wasn't careful.

After his shower, Nick stood in front of the sink, naked, shivering from his stint beneath the ice-cold water, blinking back eye drops, slicking back his wet hair.

This was a first, he thought as he gazed into the mirror. For sure, he'd had to sober up fast when faced with medical emergencies, although that hadn't happened very often in the past. But when had he ever voluntarily shrugged off the lovely, languid, lingering mists of an ancient and expensive brandy simply to focus better on a woman? What was it about Sarah Hunter that had him taking cold showers and thinking hot thoughts and praying she didn't take him for an inebriated fool in addition to an inept father?

While he dressed he called the hotel in Paris again, in the hope that Leo had awakened from his nap. This time there was no answer at all in the Davis-Finchs' suite. Nick looked at his watch. They'd gone out for dinner, no doubt, followed by fireworks and ice cream and other magical treats to make a child's eyes light up and fill his face with wonder. He made a solemn promise to himself that he was going to take Leo back there next summer, if not before.

Or, better yet...!

No. She'd never...

But perhaps she would...

Well, it couldn't hurt to ask.

He finished buttoning his shirt, and then without bothering to tuck it in or to find shoes, he headed back to the kitchen, where Sarah was plucking two slices of bread from the toaster.

"There's an eleven-fifteen flight to Paris," he said. "Why don't we go to Disneyland? Us. You and I."

Instead of answering, she dropped the hot toast on a plate, reached for a knife, and began slathering butter on each piece. Was she ignoring him?

"Sarah? Did you hear what I said?"

"Uh-huh. I heard you."

Her gaze remained fixed on the toast, as if the bread itself held some weird sort of fascination for her. He could only see her profile, but it was enough to tell that there was a tiny smile playing at the edge of her mouth. Nick took that for a positive sign.

"Well?" he asked. "What about it? What do you say? Shall we go? Tonight?"

"Well, give me just a minute, okay? I'm thinking. I'm trying to come up with a response that will humor you."

"Humor me? Why?"

"Because," she said, turning to lean against the

counter now, pointing the butter knife at him, while seemingly trying to suppress her laughter. "Well, let's see. For want of a better word, if you're not drunk anymore, then you're just plain crazy, Nick."

She twirled her index finger beside her head to emphasize her meaning. "Crazy. You know? Nuts. Bananas. A couple of screws loose. That isn't necessarily a professional diagnosis, mind you. Just a personal opinion. But one offered after quite a bit of close observation."

She turned back to her toast, slathering it with even more butter than before while she shook her head in… In what? Nick wondered. Disgust? Amusement? Complete dismissal of him?

"So, that's a no, then?" he asked, disappointed but admittedly not surprised. It was a crazy idea, the two of them flying off to Disneyland.

"Yes," she said.

Nick blinked. "It's a yes?"

"No!" She whirled around, the knife still in her hand. "You just don't understand. I'm a psychologist. I'm a very good psychologist. I'm not in Montebello on vacation. I came here to work with Leo. Not to…to…" Her voice faltered.

"To what?" he asked, believing he already knew the answer. At least, hoping he knew the answer— that she was as insanely attracted to him as he was to her—and suddenly unable to suppress a grin in anticipation of it.

"I really don't want to talk about it," she said, but the words were hardly out of her mouth before she contradicted them. "We really need to talk about this."

"All right."

She aimed a glare and the point of the knife in the direction of the table. "Sit," she said, then said it again, louder, when Nick didn't move fast enough to suit her. "Sit."

After Sarah planted herself in a chair across the table from him, she dragged in a long breath, stiffened her shoulders, and lifted her chin. When she finally started speaking, Nick quickly realized where the expression "spilling the beans" came from.

"Okay. It's really stupid not to talk about this and to clear the air. I've always thought of myself as an exceptionally rational person, someone who doesn't avoid the truth, but meets it head-on, however unpleasant it might be. I mean, uncovering unpleasant truths is part of my job. Well, not that *this* truth is so terribly unpleasant, but it certainly is complicating the current situation."

While she paused to take a breath, Nick crossed his arms and leaned back in his chair, trying hard not to look anything but seriously attentive even as he was fighting the urge to shut her up with a kiss. He had a brief glimpse of the scene in one of the Indiana Jones movies where the bad guy made a great show of brandishing his lethal scimitar, only to be casually and quite summarily plugged by Indy's .45.

"You see," Sarah continued, "I truly am a rational, clear-thinking person. I pride myself on my ability to consider the facts without letting my emotions get in the way. As a physician, Nick, I'm sure you can identify with that. Right?"

He nodded agreeably. "Of course."

"Of course," she echoed. "So I'm sure you'll understand why I'm... Well, why I've felt a little thrown off balance lately by these feelings I've been having."

"Feelings?" he asked innocently.

"About you." Sarah sagged a bit in her chair and let out a soft groan of relief. "Oh, God. It feels so good to finally get this out in the open. You know? Like the weight of the world has just been lifted from my shoulders. It's just bizarre. Like a crush, or something. This hasn't happened to me since I had the hots for Billy Dean in fourth grade. I can hardly breathe when you and I are in the same room. My heart feels as if it's turned to Silly Putty. Isn't that ridiculous?"

"Well..." he murmured in his most sober academic fashion, stroking his chin for the full effect. "Those are fairly typical physical symptoms."

"Not for me!" she wailed.

"Hmm."

It was probably time, Nick decided, for Indy to

put the poor sword-waving fellow out of his misery. To put them both out of their misery.

"I have a suggestion that might help," he said, rising out of his chair. "Stand up."

"What?" She gazed up at him without moving.

"Just stand, Sarah." He held out his hand. "You'll see."

She rose slowly, even as she murmured, "I don't know about this, Nick. What are you doing?"

"What I've wanted to do since the first moment I saw you," he said. "I'm going to kiss you."

Chapter 11

Think! Sarah warned herself.

Use your head!

Oh, the hell with it.

And those were just about the last coherent thoughts that managed to flit through her brain before she gave herself over completely to Nick's kiss. No, it was more than a kiss. She'd been kissed before, and this was nothing like anything she'd ever experienced. It was closer to a possession. An encounter of the most incredible kind.

Nick's arms encircled her so powerfully, so completely, and he held her so closely against him that it was as if they were one and the same person, or maybe Siamese twins who were joined at the lips all the way to their hips. Yes, especially the hips, where she could feel the strength of his desire through the thin fabric of her robe.

After a moment, she wasn't even breathing on her own anymore, but drawing all of her breath from him. And she was fairly sure she wasn't standing on her own, either. How could she be, when all of her bones had turned to tapioca? How could she even be thinking when her mind had softened to mush?

He smelled like expensive soap. He tasted like peppermint toothpaste with just a hint of brandy. His mouth was wonderfully cool and incredibly hot at the same time. The whiskers on his jawline made her skin tingle. All of her senses absolutely sizzled.

And how had a cat strayed into the kitchen, Sarah wondered. All of a sudden it occurred to her that the little mewing sounds she kept hearing were coming from her very own throat.

She was mewing?

Good grief.

How embarrassing.

No sooner did she begin to pull away than Nick lifted his head, breaking the kiss and easing his embrace. He didn't let her go completely, though, which was probably a good thing because she might have slid right down to the floor and lain at his feet in a warm puddle of melted flesh and bones.

"Well," she said, a little surprised at the huskiness that permeated her voice. "I don't know about you, but I certainly feel better now that we've cleared the air."

"Mmm," Nick murmured while he smiled down at her, his hands still warm on her back and the rest of him still hard against her front. "I'm glad you feel better."

"Don't you?"

"Well…" His smile turned a bit ragged at the edges. "Better? Maybe. I definitely *feel*."

Sarah took a step back, out of his arms, just to be on the safe side. "Now that these feelings are out in the open, we'll be able to deal with them like two reasonable and intelligent people."

Nick laughed as he pulled out the chair he'd been sitting in earlier. "As opposed to two unreasonable, sex-crazed people who'd rather make love than talk."

"We aren't going to make love," she told him, heading back for her cutting board and the vegetables she'd put aside when he went to shower.

"Aren't we?"

From the tone of his voice Sarah couldn't tell if he was teasing her or challenging her. Not that it made any difference.

"No, we're not," she said even more firmly. "I mean, after all, Nick, what would be the point?"

"Pleasure?"

"Fleeting pleasure," she said, picking up the knife and going at the green pepper again.

"I was thinking more along the lines of slow pleasure. Long drawn-out pleasure. Hours. Days."

Sarah rolled her eyes and clucked her tongue. "You know what I mean. It would still be nothing more than a casual fling. A quick roll in the hay."

"A leisurely roll in the hay," he corrected her.

"Whatever." She was chopping a little faster now, irritated that Nick couldn't understand what she was trying to communicate to him, that he seemed to be making a joke out of something she considered quite serious, and that even as she was spurning him, she was still enjoying the peppermint-brandy taste of him on her lips.

"I came here to work with your son, Nick. Period. Yes, I'm attracted to you."

She picked up an egg and cracked it hard on the rim of a bowl as she continued. "Yes, it's hard to breathe when you're around."

Crack. Splat.

"And, yes, that was without a doubt the most incredible kiss I have ever experienced in my entire life."

Crack. Splat.

"But so what? It's not going to happen again."

Crack. Splat.

"Ever."

Sarah picked up the bowl now and began beating the yolks and whites within an inch of their little lives, all the while feeling Nick's dark gaze on her back and knowing he was grinning like a damned pirate and probably ignoring every word she said.

"It's not going to happen again," she repeated, as much for her own ears as for Nick's.

Not if I can help it.

Oh, help!

For the next few days, in an effort to avoid Nick Chiara, Sarah nearly buried herself alive in research. After she'd consumed all the psychological journals she'd brought with her from the States, she obtained permission to use the hospital's computer to locate just about everything that had ever been written on the subject of mutism in general, and traumatic mutism in particular.

Never in her entire career had she been so strongly motivated to solve a patient's problem. And in all honesty she knew very well that the source of that motivation wasn't mere concern for the silent little boy, but her devout wish to accomplish what'd she'd come for and to get the hell out of Dodge.

"You look a little frayed at the edges, child," Lady Satherwaite said to her one afternoon when Sarah took a break from her research to visit the old woman's room.

Nick's aunt wasn't even bothering to pretend she was ill anymore, but referred to her stay in the royal wing as her "little sabbatical." By now the room was so crammed with floral arrangements, stuffed animals and Get Well Soon balloons that there was hardly anyplace for a visitor to stand or sit. Sarah had to bat a helium-filled mylar heart out of her way just to approach the bed.

"If I'm frayed at the edges, it because I've been working hard," she replied. "I think I have a much better handle on how to get Leo to speak again. I'm really anxious for him to get back from Disneyland."

"When is that? Tomorrow?"

"I think so. Nick talks to the Davis-Finches every day, hoping they'll put Leo on the phone." She sighed. "But they never do. They always come up with some sort of excuse. Either the boy's asleep, or about to go to sleep, or he's in the bathroom or brushing his teeth, or something like that."

"Morons." Lady Satherwaite gave a brusque, dismissive wave of her hand. Each day, Sarah couldn't help but notice, another ring magically appeared on her fingers. Nick must have brought them to her. That was sweet of him.

As if somehow reading Sarah's thoughts, the old woman said, "Nicky was here an hour or so ago. I must say, he doesn't look much perkier than you, dear. He seemed decidedly subdued, as a matter of fact. Is there something going on between the two of you that I ought to know about?"

"There's nothing going on," Sarah said.

It wasn't a lie, exactly. It was the absolute truth, if you didn't take into consideration the constant undercurrents of electricity that zapped between the two of them when they were in the same room, or the fact that Sarah could hardly sleep anymore, knowing Nick was only a bedroom away, wondering if he was lying awake, too, and then berating herself for wondering.

"Well, that explains it, then." Nick's aunt clasped her bejeweled hands atop her ample belly and gave a deep, disappointed sigh. "Although I can't claim to understand why the two of you are postponing the inevitable, dear. I was so in hopes that during my absence and Leo's that…"

"Whoa. That's enough." Sarah stood up, and got bopped on the head by another balloon, which she smacked aside. "You really are a meddler, Lady Satherwaite," she said, not bothering to hide her irritation. The woman wasn't ill, after all. She was just malingering and quite obviously relishing her scheme. "I don't mean to be disrespectful, but I really wish you'd go play Cupid with somebody else. I'm just not interested."

Honoria Satherwaite looked crestfallen for a second, but she obviously wasn't about to quit. "But, my dear. You said you weren't wildly in love with anyone. I distinctly remember your telling me that right here in this very room. You can't deny it."

"I don't deny it." Sarah lifted her hands in a helpless gesture as she went on. "And not only am I not wildly in love with anyone right now, but I have no intention of falling wildly in love with anyone in the future. Ever. I don't want to be wildly in love, thank you very much. I'm happy just the way I am.''

"Pish tosh. Everyone wants to fall in love. Everyone. The wilder, the better.''

Sarah shook her head adamantly. "Not me.''

"I don't believe that.''

"I'm sorry, Lady Satherwaite, but it's true. And all these schemes of yours aren't going to do anything but frustrate Nick and me, and ultimately they'll only be a terrible disappointment to you. In fact, you might just as well come home because nothing's going on there. At least, not between your nephew and me.''

"You don't find him attractive?''

"I find him incredibly attractive,'' Sarah said. "He's also intelligent and funny and kind and a hell of a kisser.''

When the old woman began to grin triumphantly and her eyes began to sparkle, Sarah quickly added, "Don't get the wrong idea now. It was just one kiss—a kind of experiment, actually—and there aren't going to be any more.''

"Well, then, you're a moron, too,'' Lady Satherwaite said.

Sarah couldn't help but laugh. "That's probably true,'' she said, "but at least I'm a moron with a purpose. And one who really needs to get back to the computer now to do some more research before

Leo gets home.'' She reached out to gently pat the
big woman's arm. ''I'll see you later.''

Honoria Satherwaite made a series of harrumphing
sounds while Sarah fought her way through a jungle
of flowers and a forest of helium balloons to get to
the door.

For several days, Nick managed to remain on his
best behavior with Sarah, which basically meant that
he took up jogging again—hard, punishing, uphill
runs, five miles in the early morning and another five
in the late afternoon. It was either that physical distraction or take half a dozen cold showers every day,
or avoid Sarah completely, which was something he
had no intention of doing. Ever.

Was he in love? The question seemed preposter-
ous, but he asked himself a hundred times a day.
He'd only just met Sarah Hunter, and he didn't believe love was possible in so short a time. He'd
known Lara Davis-Finch for at least three years before he was even willing to acknowledge that his
feelings for her were anything resembling love.

Of course, that was a long time ago and he hadn't
exactly been celibate back then. Poor Lara had had
more than a little competition. Sarah Hunter had
none. But if he wasn't in love with her, he was certainly in *something* that had his blood rampaging and
his pulse rate spiking every time he saw her.

As for her ban on kissing, Nick found himself in

complete agreement. He was fairly certain that he wouldn't be able to stop at just a kiss, and he was too out of practice to trust himself, too fearful of behaving like a fool.

His Aunt Honoria, on the other hand, was convinced not only that it was love, but that it was true love. Heaven help him. She reclined in her high bed at the hospital like some enormous goddess, gazing down from Olympus, delighting in her romantic dreams and her schemes to tamper with the tender hearts of mere mortals.

"You look simply terrible, Nicky," she said by way of a greeting when he stopped by the hospital after his afternoon jog.

"Thank you, Auntie darling." He shoved a bouquet of balloons aside in order to approach the bed, then he bent to kiss her and said, "You're looking better than ever. I've brought you the emerald pinkie ring you said you couldn't live without."

He slipped it from his little finger and onto hers, not failing to note that her hands weren't nearly as swollen as they'd been the day before. He'd changed her to a different diuretic yesterday and it seemed to be doing the trick. Other than the worrisome tendency to retain fluids, her health was excellent for a woman her age. She'd probably outlive him.

"Thank you, dear." She wiggled her finger and pondered the square-cut emerald a moment before looking back at him. "Sarah was here a little while ago."

"That's nice."

Nick braced himself for whatever it was she was going to say next. The woman could change subjects in the blink of an eye and with no apparent logic. God only knew how her mind worked. He'd lived with her for nearly three decades and he still didn't have a clue.

"We had a pleasant little chat, Sarah and I. She finds you most attractive, Nicky. And she tells me you're—oh, how did she put it?—'a hell of a kisser.' "

"That's good to hear," he said, shaking his head, then adding almost under his breath, "For what it's worth."

His aunt sat up straighter, scrunching the pillows behind her back, and then crossing her arms. "I should think it would be worth a great deal to any man, especially one who looks at a woman the way you look at Sarah Hunter."

"You're getting a bit obsessed with this, Aunt Honoria, don't you think?"

It suddenly occurred to Nick that his aunt's recent behavior truly was obsessive. Up until now, he'd written all of these ridiculous matchmaking attempts off to her inherent eccentricities and her rose-colored, romantic view of the world. But this afternoon he wasn't quite so sure. Geriatrics wasn't his specialty by any means, but he knew enough about the elderly to know that obsessive behavior could be an early symptom of dementia. Maybe he should call Doctor Helena Mancuso for a consultation.

''And don't you look at me as if I'm a crazy, bug-eyed old gypsy, Dominic Chiara,'' she snapped, obviously reading his expression correctly. ''I am not senile nor am I demented. I see what I see. And furthermore, I know what I know.''

''All right, Aunt Honoria,'' he said soothingly, reaching for her hand.

She waved him away. ''Go. Go run or whatever it is you're dressed for. I don't want to talk about this anymore, Nicky. I've done my best. I wash my hands of you both.''

He was almost out the door when he swore he heard her mutter ''Morons'' at his back.

''How's our patient?'' Sarah asked when Nick walked onto the terrace where she was reading an article she'd copied from a British psychiatric journal.

''Testy,'' he said, pulling out a chair. ''Irascible. Stubborn. Basically impossible.''

Sarah laughed. ''In other words, pretty much the same.''

''Right. She called me a moron.''

''You, too?'' She laughed again. ''Well, I guess we have a lot more in common than we thought.''

"What are you reading?" he asked, flipping the chair around and straddling it with his forearms braced over the back.

He was still in his running clothes—gray sweats and a worn pair of Reeboks. Sarah tried not to notice that he looked just as good in those as he did in a tuxedo. Maybe better.

"An article by a British psychiatrist who claims that traumatic mutism can't be cured at all without addressing the original trauma. I've been sitting here thinking how that might apply to Leo."

He sighed. "So we're back to Desmond's murder and the fire again, are we?"

She nodded. "I'm not much of a believer in co-incidence, Nick. And Leo stopped speaking right after that. There has to be a connection."

"Not if you believe Estella. And I can't think of any reason why the girl would lie. Especially when she's no longer employed by us. The truth can't get her fired."

"Even so, I'd like to talk to her again," Sarah said. "And I think I'll snoop around Desmond's place tomorrow, if that's all right."

"The police are done over there as far as I know."

"Great."

Sarah picked up her stack of articles. "Well, I think I'll take these inside and read myself to sleep."

He looked west toward the sun, which was nowhere near the horizon yet. "I don't suppose you want to have dinner with me. We could…"

"No, thanks."

She had only taken a few steps across the terrace when Nick's leg shot out to stop her.

"What are you afraid of, Sarah?" he asked, his voice low, challenge flashing in his dark eyes.

"Nothing," she said, suddenly unable to maintain eye contact for fear Nick would see something burning in her eyes, the something that kept flaming up inside her. "I'm not afraid of anything."

"Or anyone?"

"No. Not anything or anyone."

"Liar."

He lowered the barrier of his leg, allowing her to pass, and it was all Sarah—*liar, liar, pants on fire*—could do to walk, not run, into the house.

Chapter 12

The next morning, after Sarah showered and got dressed, she couldn't help but notice that the waistband of her old reliable denim skirt wasn't quite as snug as the last time she had worn it. In fact, the waistband was downright loose. By several inches. There seemed to be a little extra denim in the hips, as well.

If she hadn't known better, she'd have guessed it was somebody else's skirt, that she'd somehow packed the wrong one, perhaps her sister-in-law Kate's size ten rather than her own size eight. She even checked the sewn-in label just to make sure. It was an eight, all right, which meant that Sarah herself was now closer to a six.

Jeez.

She looked more closely in the mirror. Her sunburn from the afternoon at the Lido had turned into a decent enough tan, but her cheekbones did seem a tad more distinct, and when she rubbed beneath her eyes, hoping to discover that the darkness there was just leftover mascara, the smudges didn't disappear.

Ye gods. This wasn't good at all. She hadn't looked this thin or haggard since she'd had a bout with mono during her freshman year in college.

''It couldn't be because you've hardly eaten or slept for the past week, could it?'' she asked her emaciated reflection.

Jeez. The royal family ought to package this as a weight loss vacation. Come to lovely Montebello, where a week with one of our glamorous knights will leave you sleek and slim. They probably wouldn't want to advertise the accompanying details like insomnia or the dark circles under the eyes.

She looked at the clock beside the bed. If her own glamorous knight, Sir Dominic, held true to his recent schedule, she'd hear the front door open and close in just a minute or two, signaling that he was off for his morning jog.

A few moments later, just as she knew she would, Sarah heard the telltale click. All right! She took one last, pitiful look in the mirror, muttered a curse, then sprinted into the kitchen for a fast cup of coffee and a couple of Leo's animal crackers before she headed out the back door.

The night before, while tossing and turning, Sarah had finally arrived at the conclusion that Leo's traumatic event was the key to unlocking and hopefully curing his silence. She had become even more convinced of her theory when article after article in journal after journal offered anecdotal evidence that once a mute patient was confronted with the inciting trauma, whether the incident was actually recreated or simply talked about by the clinician, seven out of ten cases dramatically improved and the patients were speaking within a month's time.

As far as recent trauma was concerned on the palace grounds, Sarah was pretty sure there was only the murder of the king's nephew and the subsequent fire set to cover it up. She didn't believe that Leo hadn't seen it or heard it or somehow been affected by it. The child wouldn't even walk in that direction, for heaven's sake. He was definitely afraid of something.

At the end of the Chiara sidewalk, she turned right toward the palace. It was such a lovely morning with its cloudless azure sky and just a faint and salty taste of autumn coolness in the air. The huge palm fronds overhead waved and dipped gracefully in the breeze while the sun glittered and danced in every splashing fountain that she walked past. At home right now in San Francisco, the sky was probably gray with a chilly drizzle falling from it. As much as Sarah loved San Francisco, she had to admit once more that Montebello truly was a little slice of paradise.

Maybe, if her parents really did retire here in ten years or so, she'd come back for a visit. What a great idea! What fun it would be to see Leo as a tall, gangly teenager, forever yakking on the phone. If he turned out anything like his father, he'd have hearts fluttering from one end of Montebello to the other.

It would be interesting, too, to see if, in ten years time, her then almost forty-year-old heart would still do jumping jacks and somersaults at the sight of Nick Chiara. It probably would, she thought, while a silly grin worked its way across her mouth and her almost thirty-year-old heart performed a tiny pirouette.

Then Sarah could actually feel the grin slide off her face when reality suddenly jumped up and bit her. Ten years from now, if everything went as planned, she would be Mrs. Warren Dill, and her heart would be doing just what she intended it to do, which was beat steadily and dependably from one day to another, well insulated against sorrows and shocks, without suffering any roller-coaster ups and downs.

That's what she wanted, wasn't it?

Well, wasn't it?

Much to her relief, just then she turned the corner around a big hibiscus bush, saw the burned-out guest

cottage directly in front of her, and forgot to answer
her own question.

This time, instead of pondering the residence from
the safety of the sidewalk, Sarah walked across the
lawn, hopped over a boxwood shrub, and peeked in
a sooty window. As far as she could tell, it looked
as if the repair work was just getting underway.
There were two men, both of them dressed in white
T-shirts and painters' pants. One of them happened
to see her at the window and yelled something in
Italian that Sarah didn't understand.

In response, she shook her head and shrugged, a
kind of international gesture meaning "Huh?"

A moment later, when one of the painters opened
the front door and leaned out, she called to him, "I
was just looking. Just curious. Would it be possible
for me to come inside?"

"Inside?" he echoed.

"Yes. Yes, please. *Por favor,* signor. I'd like to
come inside. Just for a few minutes." She pointed to
herself and then over his shoulder, gesturing inside
the guest cottage, and hoping like hell he didn't take
it personally and translate the gesture as *Me, Jane—
You, Tarzan.* But the painter apparently did understand her gesture because he immediately scowled
and shook his head.

"No, signorina. *Polizia.*" He pointed toward a
banner of yellow tape fluttering beside the door.

"Polizia," he said again, a little louder. "No come in. *Scusa.*"

"But…"

The painter stepped back inside and slammed the door, putting an end to any negotiation.

Nuts. She dearly wished she knew how to say that in Italian, or better yet some other, preferably stronger expletive to communicate her disappointment.

Oh, well. Sarah took one final peek through the window. She doubted that she'd find anything inside the guest cottage now anyway that would give her any kind of clue about Leo. She didn't need a vacant residence. What she needed was an eyewitness, one a whole lot more forthcoming than Estella, the nanny.

Not knowing just what to do next, she wandered toward a stone bench not too far from the cottage. There, she sat and hiked up the hem of her skirt just a few inches above her knees to get a little more color on her legs.

Every once in a while, she turned to look at the vacant residence behind her.

You never knew, she thought. They said the criminal always came back to the scene of his crime. It had been almost a month now since Desmond Caruso's murder, but still…

And just as that rather grisly thought was crossing her mind, a pair of hands suddenly covered Sarah's eyes and a voice, very Italian and oddly familiar, exclaimed *"Cara mia!"*

Sarah shrieked, wrenching away the hands that were blinding her, and then turned to face Estella's ardent and once again misguided suitor, Bruno.

"Aiee," he said, slapping his forehead with the heel of his hand. *"Scusa,* signorina. I thought you were Estella. We used to come here. To this chair." He pointed to the bench on which Sarah sat.

Sarah blinked. "You and Estella used to come here?"

Bruno nodded. "Always. *Si.* Many times."

"While she was working at the Chiara house?"

"Si." He looked at the ground and shrugged. "There was no other time to be together. Her father...um..."

"Disapproved," Sarah suggested, recalling the angry male voice at Estella's apartment.

"Si. Her father disapproved. How do you say...big time?"

"Yeah. That's how you say it," she replied while her curiosity increased big time. "What did Estella do with Leo while the two of you were here? Did she sneak out to meet you while he was taking his nap?"

"The *bambino?* He come. Estella took good care of him. She would not leave him. He come with us on his bicycle or with his toys. Sometimes he visit..."

Bruno's mouth snapped closed almost audibly, as if he suddenly realized he was about to say something he shouldn't.

"It's okay, Bruno," Sarah said quickly. "Estella's not in any trouble. She did a fine job with the boy. But tell me who Leo visited." She looked over her shoulder, back at the guest cottage. "Was it the man who lived there?"

Bruno glanced at the cottage and then nodded rather sheepishly. "*Si.* The bambino and Signor Caruso, they play checkers, other games. They laugh sometimes. Sing. Joke. Many laughs."

Oh my God, Sarah thought. Oh, my God. Leo and the dead man were pals. Buddies. Nick and his aunt probably had absolutely no idea that Estella was sneaking out with Bruno and letting the little boy wander around on his own. This might very well be the explanation she'd been searching for. It had to be. This was the trauma! Leo found out that his friend, Desmond, was dead and the poor little boy— out of shock, sorrow or fear—stopped speaking.

She shot up from the bench so fast it startled Bruno, who jumped back a foot or two.

"You know that the man who lived there was murdered, don't you, Bruno?" she asked.

He sighed and glanced at the cottage again. "*Si. Aiee.* That happen the day before my boat leave. Sad."

"Then I guess Estella had to tell Leo that his friend was dead. Did she tell him?"

"No."

Bruno's reply was instantaneous and offered with absolute certainty, but at the same time Sarah noticed that his gaze wavered from hers. The fact that the man couldn't maintain eye contact with her was a pretty clear indication that he was lying, so she asked again, this time a bit more urgently.

"Did Estella tell Leo that Desmond Caruso was dead? I need to know, Bruno. Please tell me the truth. It's very important."

His gaze flitted off again. "Oh, signorina…"

"You won't get in trouble if you tell me," she said. "Neither you nor Estella. I promise you. This is just between us. But I need to find out exactly what happened."

To emphasize her seriousness, Sarah clasped Bruno's arm just above the elbow. "Did you know that Leo hasn't spoken a word since Desmond Caruso died? Not a single word. I came all the way from the United States in order to help him speak again, but I can't help him at all if you won't tell me the truth."

His eyes met hers now. "I did not know. The *bambino* does not speak? This is terrible, no? Not good. Not good."

"No, it isn't good at all." She tightened her grip on his arm, and stepped a bit closer. "But with your help, I know I can get the little boy to speak again and be happy again. Please, Bruno. Tell me. Did Estella tell Leo that his friend, Desmond, was dead?"

"No. No, signorina. She did not have to tell him."

"Excuse me?"

"The *bambino*… He…" Bruno drew in a long breath, then let it out as he said, "He saw his friend dead."

"He saw…" Sarah's hand went from Bruno's arm to her own astonished mouth. All of a sudden she felt light headed, so she sat back down on the stone bench, murmuring, "Oh, my God. Leo saw the body. Oh, that poor child. No wonder."

"He saw more," Bruno said solemnly, lowering himself beside her. He lowered his voice, too, as he leaned closer to Sarah closer and whispered, "Signorina, he saw more. I believe he saw the murder."

She could only stare at him now.

"The boy, he ran to us. He was crying." Bruno pointed to his own eyes. "Big tears. So, we go with him to the house and we see the man, the blood. *Aiee.* Terrible. Terrible."

"And you didn't tell anyone?" Sarah asked.

"Me, I want to tell the *polizia* right away. But Estella…" He shook his head. "Too afraid to lose her job, you know? Afraid of Sir Dominic and the big lady. Afraid of her papa most of all. So I promise her not to talk. And Leo, he promise her, too."

"What do you mean, Leo promised her?"

Bruno started looking sheepish again. In fact, Sarah thought he looked pretty damned guilty, which he certainly was for not doing anything to alert the authorities about the murder while agreeing to let a child suffer its aftereffects all alone, with no one to console him or explain what had happened to his friend.

"What did Leo promise?" she asked again.

"Not to talk. He promise not to talk to anyone. Estella tell him that if he talks, the bad person will come back and hurt him. If he say one word, then maybe the bad person try to kill him, too."

"Oh, my God," Sarah moaned, suddenly understanding what had happened. She never would have guessed. "Estella told him not to talk about the murder, but the poor baby must have taken it literally and thought she was ordering him not to talk at all."

No wonder he was silent! It all made perfect sense now. Perfect, horrible sense. Poor Leo thought he'd be murdered, just like his pal Desmond, if he made even a single peep. Talk about a traumatic experience! And it wasn't even in the past. The poor little kid was still living under a death threat. Even now.

She jumped up from the bench. "Thank you, Bruno. You've helped more than you can imagine. *Grazie.*"

Sarah turned to race back to the Chiara cottage, but Bruno caught her hand.

"Signorina, you promised to tell me where to find

my Estella," he said. "*Por favor,* Signorina. Where is she?"

Grateful as she was for the information he'd just given her, Sarah wasn't about to reward the man who'd been partially responsible for Leo's silence.

"I don't know," she lied, pulling away from him. "Sorry. Thank you again, Bruno. I really have to go now."

"But, Signorina..." he protested.

"Sorry."

Sarah took off at a lope for Nick's place with Bruno on her heels like a sad-faced, Italian blood-hound.

On his morning jogs, Nick habitually made a wide circuit of the old part of San Sebastian before turning back toward the palace. On King Augustus Avenue, a few blocks from the quay, he always paused for a minute or two in front of the building where he and his aunt had lived when he was growing up. He'd tell himself he was just stopping to catch his breath, but the truth was that he enjoyed those moments of nostalgia, gazing at the stucco-fronted Number 24 with its wrought iron balconies and blossom-laden window boxes.

The little café on the ground floor was still run by the Rendazzi family. Their cats still basked in the sunshine of the doorway, and the smell of the es-presso machine still wafted out onto the sidewalk, luring in pedestrians. Amazingly enough, when Nick looked up, the window box on the second floor apartment was planted with pink geraniums, just as it had been when he and Aunt Honoria had resided there all those years ago.

Sometimes it seemed as if nothing in Montebello ever changed. Sometimes it seemed as if everything changed in the blink of an eye. He'd gone from husband to father to widower in what seemed like a heartbeat. One day Leo was laughing and talking nonstop; the next day his son was silent. Now Sarah Hunter had come into his life and Nick had the feeling that, whatever happened between them, things would never be the same for him again.

He cursed himself then for letting his thoughts turn toward the woman he was running to avoid thinking about. Better to fill his brain with work, to contemplate the clinical trials for a new analgesic the hospital would soon undertake, to organize his thoughts about the proposed expansion to the surgical wing, or decide whether or not he should remain the palace physician, allowing his own surgical skills to atrophy while he tended to the queen's migraines and the king's ulcer and Prince Lucas's rehabilitation.

While he negotiated the traffic on the broad Avenida Media, he did his best to clear his head of everything but the feel of the pavement beneath his feet and the warmth of the sun on his face. Then he turned onto the palace grounds, was waved through by the guard, and continued on the path toward home, walking now, cooling down.

Then, almost home, Nick turned a landscaped corner and, not too far away, saw Sarah being chased by some slick-haired, T-shirted, weight-lifting Romeo.

Every synapse in his body seemed to fire instantaneously as he raced to her rescue.

Chapter 13

Sarah considered herself a pretty good runner, even at the ripe old age of twenty-nine. Her jewelry box at home still held the medal she'd won in high school for the four hundred meter relay. It helped that she did her jogging—when she got around to doing it these days—on the hilly, sometimes torturous streets of San Francisco. Considering all that, she'd been fairly sure that, once she took off, she'd leave the muscle-bound Bruno in the royal dust.

But it hadn't happened that way. The guy was relentless. Apparently his desire to obtain Estella's address and to see the nanny again had put wings on Bruno's sandaled feet.

The Chiara place was still a good hundred yards

away when Sarah decided the race wasn't worth the stitch in her side or the sweat that was starting to soak through her shirt. She'd give her pursuer the nanny's stupid address. What did it matter anyway?

Then, at the same instant that she decided to slow down, Bruno apparently decided to speed up. He crashed into her with his full two hundred plus pounds at thirty miles per hour, and Sarah went wind-milling forward and then sprawling onto the perfectly clipped royal grass.

She wasn't really clear on what happened in the next few seconds. There was a lot of shouting above her, but since it was in Italian she couldn't understand much of what was said, except for a few explicit four-letter words that were pretty much the same in any language. There was some scuffling of feet and several deep-throated grunts followed by more four-letter words.

Then, while she struggled to get up from the ground, she heard the sound of retreating footsteps, and the next thing she knew she was five feet off the ground in Nick Chiara's arms.

She didn't like to be babied or coddled—that just wasn't acceptable in her family, where if you fell, you got up and went on. End of story. As a result of her upbringing, her first instinct was to push away from the solid chest against which she found herself pressed.

On second thought, there was that wonderful underlying soap smell that was so Nick, and now it was mixed with a healthy, athletic dose of masculine sweat. And there was his warm breath against her hair and the brush of his whiskery jaw against the side of her face, not to mention the oh-so-marvelous, warm, and suddenly safe feeling of simply being in this man's arms.

For one lovely second, Sarah allowed herself not only to savor it, but to wish for more. Much, much more.

"*Cara*," he said softly, his lips against her hair. "Are you all right, Sarah?"

"Mmm."

"Are you all right?" he asked again.

"Mmm."

Oh, lord. She sounded as if she were about to start that awful mewing again, so Sarah cleared her throat and said, "You should probably put me down now, Nick."

He simply looked at her then, his face just inches away from hers, and his expression was so sad and so adorable. As deeply disappointed as a little kid who'd just been told that Christmas had been cancelled. As dejected as a knight in shining armor who'd just discovered he'd rescued the wrong damsel in distress.

And when it suddenly dawned on Sarah that Sir Dominic Chiara really was a genuine, twenty-four-karat, card-carrying knight, she burst out laughing.

"Nick, put me down," she managed to say.

"Are you sure you're all right?"

"I'm positive."

Still holding her, he frowned. "What's so funny? And who was that maniac and why was he chasing you?"

"That was Bruno, and he…"

Sarah stopped giggling as she remembered why she'd been running toward the house in the first place. She'd been rushing to tell Nick what she'd learned about Leo and the murder of Desmond Caruso.

"Okay. Put me down now. I mean it," she said in all seriousness. "I've got something really important to tell you."

"And you believe this guy? This Bruno?" Nick asked as he poured a finger of brandy into a snifter. It was pretty early in the day for a drink, but he wasn't on call and it wasn't every day a man discovered that his son might be a witness to an unsolved murder.

"Yes, I do," Sarah said. She was nestled in a corner of the sofa in the living room with her legs curled up beneath her. "He has absolutely no reason to lie about this, Nick. In fact, just telling the truth could get old Bruno in plenty of hot water. Not just with Estella and her father, but with the authorities, as well. It would've been in his best interest not to tell me anything at all, you know.''

Nick sipped the brandy as he lowered himself onto the sofa beside her, nodding but still not entirely convinced about what Sarah had told him.

''Why are you so skeptical?'' she asked him, clearly reading the expression on his face.

''Well, in the first place, I have a rather hard time picturing Desmond Caruso spending any time at all with a child, someone who couldn't benefit him financially or socially. The man wasn't exactly what you'd call a Pied Piper.'' He gave his brandy a quick swirl before adding, ''Viper was more like it, actually.''

''Well, Leo's an adorable little kid. Maybe Desmond wasn't quite the snake you thought he was.''

Nick shrugged. In addition to his skepticism about the murdered man, he might also have added his own disappointment that his son apparently hadn't trusted him enough to come forward with the truth about seeing Desmond dead. Of course, he hadn't actually asked Leo, had he? He'd asked the nanny instead, and hadn't for a moment considered that Estella might be lying to him.

When would he ever learn? Nick gazed into the swirling liqueur in the snifter as he warmed it in his palm, reminding himself that, after Lara had deceived him by hiding her illness, he'd vowed never to trust a woman again. He hadn't been too successful in carrying out that vow. He'd believed the nanny implicitly, hadn't he?

Hell, he even believed what Sarah was telling him right now. But this was Sarah. He didn't think she had a deceitful bone in her entire, and quite lovely, body.

"If it's true," he said, "what do we do? About getting Leo to speak, I mean."

"I'm not sure yet. If this all began with Estella ordering Leo not to talk, then the ideal solution, of course, would be to arrange for Estella to simply tell Leo that it's okay to talk now. *Voila.*" She snapped her fingers. "All cured!"

Nick sighed. "If only it were as simple as that."

"When is he coming home from Disneyland? Tomorrow?"

"Tomorrow afternoon," he said. "Which reminds me. I need to call the dreaded Davis-Finches to find out what time their flight arrives."

"Well, that gives us a little more than twenty-four hours to come up with some sort of plan. It'll work, Nick. I'm sure of it. And probably pretty quickly, too, now that we know the reason for his silence. In fact, I should probably get in touch with the dreaded Sophia at the palace to arrange my flight home."

While Nick went to place a call to his in-laws in Paris, Sarah stayed in her corner of the sofa, staring off into space, absently chewing on a fingernail. She was thinking about her flight back to San Francisco. For somebody who hadn't wanted to come to Montebello in the first place, she was suddenly and strangely depressed by the mere idea of leaving.

This wasn't good, she thought. This wasn't good at all. As a psychologist, she was quick to identify mood changes and emotional swings in others, but she rarely, if ever, suffered such extremes herself. She was reliably even-tempered. Good old Sarah Sunshine. That's who she was. That's who she'd always been. Now, all of a sudden, she felt like Temperamental Tess.

Going back to San Francisco meant returning to her patients at the clinic, which pleased her, but it also meant going back to Warren Dill. It meant making wedding plans. Worse—Sarah rolled her eyes—it meant actually having to marry him at some point.

Going back to San Francisco meant she wouldn't be here to carry out Leo's therapy or to oversee the person who did. Not that she'd mentioned it to Nick yet, but identifying the cause of Leo's problem was just the beginning, after all. There would still be a great deal of work to do to ensure that there was no emotional fallout or long-term damage from what the little boy had seen. Plus they still didn't know if he'd only seen the body, or if he'd indeed witnessed the crime. That would make an enormous difference in his treatment.

And then there was Nick.

She could hear his voice in the kitchen right now as he spoke with Leo's grandmother, and she marveled that in just a week's time that voice had become so familiar to her, so soothing and at the same time so exciting. His English was flawless, but there was always that sensuous Italian undertone, a slight Continental cadence in every sentence that Nick spoke. She loved listening to him.

Funny. Sarah couldn't for the life of her recall Warren's voice right now. Wait. That wasn't quite true. She could hear the way he always answered his phone. *Hallo.* He never said hello for some odd reason. It was always a quick, nasal, irritating *Hallo.*

Oh, God. Did she really plan to wake up every morning for the rest of her life to have the man on the other side of the bed turn to her and say *Hallo?* The mere thought of hearing that horrible greeting 365 days a year for years on end sent a shiver down her spine.

Of course, she wasn't marrying Warren because she was enamoured of his voice or because she was wildly in love with him. She was marrying him specifically because she *wasn't* wildly in love with him. That was the plan, and she'd actually been pretty proud of herself for coming up with it and for choosing a life's companion with her head rather than her heart.

The same heart, as a matter of fact, that began to go from zero to sixty in the blink of any eye now that she saw Nick coming back into the living room, moving with a masculine grace that made it impossible for her to take her eyes off him.

He was carrying the phone, and when he held it out to her, he said, "It's the King. For you."

"Me?" Sarah was torn. Part of her felt like genuflecting as she took the receiver. Most of her felt like saying "Not now. Tell His Majesty I'll call him back." Lucky for her, good manners prevailed over lust.

Lucky for her, too, King Marcus kept the conversation brief. She updated him on Leo's progress, sounding a lot more optimistic than she felt.

"I spoke to your father in San Francisco this morning," the king said. "He said to tell you all is well."

"That's good."

"I won't keep you, Sarah dear. If there's anything you need from the palace, please contact Albert, my private secretary. Signorina Strezzi is no longer with us. Some unfortunate brouhaha over Nick's bronze medal. I don't know the details."

Sarah almost laughed. *Arrivederci* Sophia.

After she broke the connection, she looked back at Nick.

If he weren't so damned handsome… If his almost black eyes didn't shine whenever he looked at her… If his mouth didn't do that marvelous little half hitch just before he grinned… If he were stupid and in-sensitive, instead of brilliant and kind…

If he hadn't scooped her up from the grass earlier today and somehow made her feel safer than she'd ever felt before in her entire life… Because how well she knew that feeling so safe was simply an illusion. She'd seen her brother, Elliot, safe and happy that way only to have his life ripped apart when his wife and child were killed. She was sure the same thing would happen one sad day in the future when the first of her parents passed away, leaving the other one distraught and in emotional ruins.

It had happened to Nick when his wife died.

And Sarah had vowed that it would never happen to her.

Never.

That sort of pain, that magnitude of loss and grief, just wasn't worth the risk.

Only now…

Nobody should look as good in ratty gray sweats as he did in a tuxedo. Nobody should tamper with the rhythms of her heart, making her feel like a prime candidate for a pacemaker.

"They're sending Leo home by himself tomor-row," Nick said, settling onto the sofa. "Roger's been called back to London for a meeting or some-thing."

"All by himself?" she asked. "Is that a good idea?"

"I offered to come to Paris in the morning to get him, but they've hired the female concierge at their hotel to accompany him. She and Leo have struck up a friendship, I gather, and it's a short flight. He'll arrive at two o'clock."

"I'd like to go with you to the airport tomorrow," she said. "Not just to welcome Leo back, but I could probably pick up a ticket there for my flight home. There's really no need to bother anyone at the palace about it."

She sounded casual enough, but the thought of leaving Montebello almost made her sick. No. Not leaving Montebello. It was the thought of leaving Nick.

He reached out to touch her cheek. "*Cara,* what is it? What's wrong? You look so sad."

There was such concern in his expression as he gazed at her, and Sarah could have sworn that Nick's dark eyes were now glossy with tears. It was nearly impossible not to throw her arms around him and kiss him.

"Nothing's wrong. Nothing. Really."

She sighed, unwound her legs and got up from the sofa, anxious to put a bit of distance between herself and temptation, and at the same time wanting to curl up on Nick's lap and begin purring like a kitten and beg him not to let her go.

But before she could step away, Nick stood up, too, and caught her in his arms.

"Oh, don't," she said, only in some bizarre way when the caution came out of her mouth, it sounded more like an invitation.

"Don't what?" he whispered. "This?" He moved one hand upward, warmly, slowly, curling his fingers around her neck, sending a shock wave of longing through her whole body.

"Or this?"

The arm that still circled her waist drew her even closer against him. Sarah could almost feel her temperature go up a few degrees while her senses began to reel from the nearness of his mouth and the warm brandied fragrance of his breath and the solid heat of his chest, which she could feel through the fabric of his gray sweats, and the hard heat of him pressing against her a bit further down.

"Or this?"

He kissed one corner of her mouth, and then the other side. In between, he gently teased the seam of her lips with his tongue.

"Or this?" he whispered just before he covered her mouth with his own.

In that moment, something in Sarah broke. Some wall came tumbling down. Or maybe, since her head didn't seem to be functional anymore, her heart had finally gained control.

As her mouth opened to accept Nick's kiss, it felt as if the rest of her opened, as well.

Suddenly, with Nick, she was prepared to take the

risk. Ready to leap and to believe his strong arms would be there to catch her.

Without breaking their kiss, those strong arms swept her up and Sarah held on for dear life.

Chapter 14

"Sarah. My sweet darling Sarah."

Nick grazed the palm of his hand over her smooth, warm flank. After they'd made love, she had sighed luxuriously, rolled onto her side and nestled into him like a spoon, with her lovely, luscious rump tucked into his groin.

"The next time, my love," he whispered into her warm hair, "we'll go for endurance rather than intensity."

She sighed again, a sated, deeply satisfied sound. "There's a lot to be said for intensity."

"Amen to that."

He wasn't sure if it had been Sarah herself, or the electric culmination of five years of celibacy, or a heart-stopping combination of both, but Nick Chiara had never before experienced a sexual climax in every single cell of his body. From the soles of his feet to the top of his head, his entire body had exploded a moment ago, leaving him temporarily blind and deaf and absolutely dumbstruck.

"You cried out something in Italian, Nick," Sarah murmured. "What was it?"

He hadn't the vaguest idea. "Begging for mercy, probably," he answered only half in jest. He was an experienced man, but in all his experience no woman had ever matched him thrust for thrust the way Sarah did. No woman had ever fit him so perfectly or sheathed him like a glove. No one had ever pushed him over the edge the way this woman just had.

When his fingers stilled on her hip, Sarah reached for his hand and drew it around to her breast.

"I was actually hoping it wouldn't be good between us, Nick," she said. "I was even hoping I'd be disappointed. Completely and totally turned off." She laughed softly. "I was hoping you'd have horrible warts all over your body and gross hair all over your back and a teeny, weenie..."

Hard again, he thrust against the soft cleavage of her backside. Her voice drifted off in a soft moan.

"Sorry to disappoint you, love," he murmured.

Sarah shifted her weight beneath his arm, and rolled back to face him. Her cheeks were still flushed and her chin a little chafed from his beard. Her green eyes were glistening almost playfully, while a slow smile spread across her mouth and she reached a hand down between their bodies to find him, to caress him.

"Disappoint me again, Nick," she breathed. "Now."

They missed lunch and dinner, and finally— around eight that evening, ravenous for more than each other—Sarah and Nick reluctantly got out of bed and into the shower, where their slick, soapy bodies couldn't help but collide once again as warm water beat down on them.

"You're an animal," Sarah had said, laughing as water cascaded over her shoulders.

"What kind?" he asked.

"My kind."

It was nearly midnight when they finally put on robes and went to the kitchen for something to eat.

"You're about to discover, Sir Dominic, that not only am I great in bed, but I also make the world's best grilled cheese sandwich." Sarah spoke as she pulled cheese and butter and a jar of Dijon mustard from the refrigerator.

She kept marveling at the fact that, rather than being exhausted by hours of lovemaking, her energy level felt boundless. It was as if she were breathing pure oxygen.

And it wasn't just the sex!

As much as they'd made love, she and Nick had spent at least an equal amount of time talking about anything and everything. Like children on a sleepover, sharing secrets. Like two people in a lifeboat, sharing hopes and dreams. They'd spoken about Leo, Lady Satherwaite, her parents, pets they'd both had decades ago, favorite foods, worst fears, recurrent dreams and silly jokes.

It was as if they were trying to catch up on a lifetime of knowing each other in a single night. More than that, it was as if their hearts and their souls had always belonged to each other, and now their minds and their bodies were simply catching up.

Now, standing at the kitchen counter, buttering slices of bread while Nick poured orange juice for them, Sarah felt so alive and so damned happy, she could hardly keep her feet upon the floor.

"This is insane," she said, almost to herself. "People don't fall in love and make lifetime decisions in a few hours. Do they?"

"Apparently they do, darling." Nick handed her a glass of orange juice, then clinked his glass against hers in a toast. "If this isn't love, Sarah, I don't know what else it could be."

He lifted her hair and kissed the back of her neck, whispering endearments in Italian. Sarah didn't need to know the language to know he'd just told her he loved her. It wasn't the first time tonight that he'd proclaimed it in English and Italian both.

"I think we ought to slow down, Nick," she said. "Don't you?"

Sarah took a thoughtful sip from her glass, wondering whether she actually wanted him to agree with her or ached for him to tell her that slowing down was terrible idea while he dragged her back to the bedroom. When he didn't answer, she wasn't sure he'd even heard her, so she asked again.

"What do you think, Nick? Maybe we're rushing way too fast. Maybe... Oh, I don't know. We really ought to be using our heads here. Maybe I should go home for a few weeks and see if we both still feel the same after a little time. That would be the sane thing to do. The reasonable thing. Don't you agree?"

When Nick still failed to respond, Sarah looked over her shoulder to see him sitting at the table. A dark look of caution had suddenly come over his handsome face.

"I'll still feel the same," he said. "Tomorrow. Next week. Next year."

"Yes, but..."

"I want you, Sarah. In my bed. In my life. In my heart."

"Yes, but..."

"Why are you so afraid to love me?"

"I'm not," she wailed.

But she knew it was a lie even as she said it. And by now she knew Dominic Chiara well enough to know that there was nothing he hated more than deceit. That look of caution was still on his face, and now, as she studied the expression, it struck her as bordering on fear.

Poor Nick, she thought. He was sitting there trying to be patient, trying to understand her feelings, and at the same time he was scared to death that she was talking herself right out of his bed and his life and his heart.

It suddenly dawned on Sarah that as much as she was afraid of getting hurt herself, she had it in her power to hurt Nick just as much. He knew it. And now she realized it, too. She could read the fear in his dark eyes. And yet it didn't keep him from taking the risk. It didn't prevent him from putting his heart in her hands and trusting it to her care. Come what may.

Whatever defenses remained inside her, Sarah could almost feel them tumbling down. But instead of leaving her empty, as she had always feared, love moved in to take their place. Love and trust and unspeakable joy.

She swallowed the lump that was gathering in her throat, and spoke as clearly as her trembling lips would allow.

"I was afraid, Nick. Oh, God, I was so afraid to risk my heart. To risk *me*. But I'm not anymore. I'm not."

Then she rushed into his arms, laughing and crying at the same time, saying "I love you, Nick Chiara. I

love you. I love you. I love you'' over and over
again.

Neither one of them got a wink of sleep that night,
so it didn't come as much of a surprise to Nick that,
when he and Sarah stopped by the hospital on the
way to the airport, his aunt took one look at them,
rolled her pale blue eyes melodramatically and muttered something about the wisdom of moderation.

Nick stood in the doorway and laughed. "It's all
your fault, you know, you wicked gypsy."

"Pish tosh." She waved them in with a fully
ringed hand. "Don't just dawdle on the threshold.
Come in. Come in. Might I suggest a small wedding
on the terrace? Sarah, dear, how much notice will
your family require? It would be delightful if we
could arrange this before the weather turns in November."

"We'll probably elope," Nick told her. "Sorry to
disappoint you, darling."

She rolled her eyes again. "You sound just like
your father."

"We've got wonderful news for you, Lady Satherwaite," Sarah told her as Nick cleared a path for
her through the jungle of balloons. "News about
Leo."

Her gypsy expression turned serious and she sat
up straighter in the high bed. "He's speaking! Oh,
please, please, tell me he's speaking again."

"Well, not yet," Sarah said, edging a hip onto the bed. "But he will. I can almost certainly promise you that. We found out yesterday that Estella had been sneaking out to meet her boyfriend with Leo in tow."

While she continued to explain about the nanny and Bruno and the late Desmond, Nick settled into a chair by the window, closed his eyes, and listened to the voices of the two women he loved. He'd never known a woman as forthright and honest as Sarah Hunter.

Even before they'd made love the first time yesterday, she'd jumped up from his bed, paced the room for a moment, and then blurted out all in a single breath, "There's something you need to know, Nick. I was supposed to marry a man named Warren Dill, only I've broken our engagement. He just doesn't know it yet."

The first thing she'd done this morning—well, actually the *second* thing—was place a call to her erstwhile fiancé in San Francisco to give him the bad news. Then, after a brief, blunt conversation, she'd hung up laughing.

"What's so funny?" Nick had asked.

"Warren." Still chuckling, she'd shaken her head. "I couldn't tell if he was devastated or not. All he said was that I ought to be very, very sure of this decision, especially considering the tax consequences of living in Montebello."

"We'll live anywhere you want, Sarah," Nick had told her. "Here. San Francisco. Anywhere."

"It doesn't matter. As long as I'm with you. With you and Leo." And then her pretty face had lit up like an American Fourth of July, and she'd exclaimed, "Oh, Nick! I'm going to be a mother."

He looked at his watch. It was time to leave for the airport to meet his son's plane. Nick couldn't wait to give him the good news.

One advantage to living in Montebello, Sarah thought as she followed Nick through a private security entrance at the airport, was that she'd never have to wait in line at an airport again. Being close to royalty wasn't such a bad deal, really.

Being close to her knight was the best deal in the world. She linked her arm through his as they turned down the wide corridor of the terminal. Because she'd arrived on the Sebastiani's private plane, she hadn't seen this part of the airport before.

Up ahead, through a wide sweep of window, she could see an airliner taxiing up to a jetway.

"He's on time," Nick said, walking a little faster.

Sarah's heart edged up into her throat. This time when she looked at Leo, she'd be seeing her soon-to-be, very own son. Nick couldn't wait to tell him the news, but suddenly Sarah felt that, on top of everything else, it might overwhelm the poor kid.

"Nick." She slowed down. "Let's wait a little

while before we say anything about us. Let's wait until we get a better handle on this Desmond thing. Maybe even until Leo starts talking again. I know you can't wait to tell him, but don't do it right now. Please. Trust me on this.''

"If you think so.'' He sounded disappointed, even as he agreed.

They stood so close, awaiting Leo's arrival, that Sarah was pretty sure, whether they told the boy or not, they wouldn't fool him for a second. Children knew when people were in love, sometimes even before adults caught on.

"There he is,'' Nick said just as Leo's dark mop of hair and sweet, smiling face appeared in the jetway.

He started running toward them, but after a few steps the boy stopped dead in his tracks and his eyes grew huge with fear.

Sarah's heart lurched. "Oh, Nick. Something's wrong.''

Then Leo screamed and pointed. "There she is! I see her! I see her! It's the bad lady who hurt my friend.''

Chapter 15

Nick turned immediately in the direction his son was pointing to see a woman quickly disappearing through the moving tide of passengers. He glimpsed her profile, got a fleeting impression of her face as she blended in with the crowd. Her hair was blond and wavy. He guessed she was a little over five feet tall and weighed about one hundred fifteen pounds. In her thirties, probably. And he thought she looked vaguely familiar somehow.

Although he longed to embrace his son, Nick sensed that it was crucial right now to prevent the suspect from getting away, and since Leo was in Sarah's capable and loving hands, he shouldered his way through the crowd in pursuit.

Her blonde head appeared and then disappeared among the tide of passengers. He was afraid he was losing her. If she managed to get aboard a plane, what then?

Nick grabbed the first uniformed shoulder he saw. He described the woman to the airport security guard, who said he would alert his superiors. A moment later the P.A. system blared the suspect's description, asking everyone to report it immediately if they spotted her. Uniformed officers began swarming through the terminal.

Feeling he'd done the best he could under the circumstances, Nick headed back to the gate.

Sarah was kneeling beside Leo, her voice soft and reassuring over the sound of his sobbing. "Oh, it's all right, sweetheart. You're safe. She isn't going to hurt you."

Leo looked up. "Papa!"

He nearly leapt into his father's arms, and Nick couldn't hold him close enough, couldn't kiss the boy's wet face enough, couldn't tell him he was loved and safe enough. His voice was clogged with emotion when he said again and again, "I love you, Leo. Papa loves you. You're safe, son. It's all right."

A moment later, Sarah put her hand on his arm. "I just talked to the woman who flew with him from Paris. She'll take the next plane back. Let's get him out of here, Nick. Let's go home."

* * *

On the drive back to the palace from the airport, Leo sat on Sarah's lap and it wasn't long before his tears stopped. Thank God five-year-olds were easy to distract.

And this five-year-old, now that he'd started speaking again, sounded as if he'd never quit.

"Tell me all about Disneyland," Sarah had said, and the little boy launched into a ten minute monologue about Mickey and Goofy and every single one of the Seven Dwarfs.

Behind the steering wheel, Nick just grinned. "I'd almost forgotten the sound of his voice after all this time. Or the breadth of his vocabulary."

Just that moment Leo said, "Actually, I liked Sneezy best. Actually, I like you, too, Sarah."

She laughed and hugged him. "Actually, I like you, too, Leo."

"Will you always be my nanny?" he asked.

"Yes, sweetheart." She longed to tell him that she would be so much more than just his nanny, but Sarah knew it was best to wait with that amazing bit of news.

By the time they reached the palace, Leo was fast asleep on Sarah's lap.

Nick carried him inside and tucked him into bed.

"Let's leave the light on," Sarah said. "I wouldn't want him to wake up later in the dark and not know where he is. Poor baby."

After they tiptoed out, Nick immediately called the

police, who insisted he come to headquarters to provide them with a description of the woman Leo had seen.

While he was gone, Sarah called the hospital to tell Lady Satherwaite what had happened.

"Oh, my dear. That's the best news I've heard all day," Nick's aunt exclaimed. "I can't wait to put my arms around the child. When Nicky's done with the police, Sarah dear, have him come and sign me out of here, will you?"

"I'll be happy to. It'll be nice to have everybody home."

"Indeed. And I've been thinking about that. Didn't you tell me your father owns some property on the coast north of San Sebastian?"

"Yes. At least I believe it's north. Several acres, if I remember correctly."

"Isn't that divine?" Lady Satherwaite sighed. "I must call your parents and tell them what a perfectly wonderful wedding gift that will be for you and Nicky. Then we'll meet with Emilio Mira, the architect who did the latest addition to the palace. He's brilliant even if he is a bit deaf. Oh, Sarah. We're going to have such fun."

Actually, Sarah thought, it did sound like fun. Lady Satherwaite was still going on about architects and landscaping and interior design when Nick got back from the police station.

"Who are you talking to?" he asked, lowering himself wearily onto the sofa beside her.

Sarah didn't answer. She merely held out the phone and listened as Honoria Satherwaite's chatter filled the space between them. "Now I know where Leo gets it," she said with a laugh, handing Nick the phone.

"Hello, darling," he said, and then "No, I'm not sending a car to collect you this evening. I'll pick you up myself tomorrow. Why? Because Leo's asleep and I'm about to take Sarah to bed. That's why." He grinned. "Yes, I thought you'd see the sense in that. I'll see you tomorrow, love."

He broke the connection and tossed the phone aside, then pulled Sarah into his arms. "It's been a long day," he said with a deep sigh.

"What happened with the police?" she asked, maneuvering one arm so she could massage his neck.

"We came up with a police sketch of the woman. I believe Leo pointed to at the airport. I'm not sure how accurate it is, but when the police brought it to the palace, Prince Lucas actually thought the woman looked familiar. The police are going to publicize the picture, see if anyone turns her in. They'll want Leo to look at it, but I got them to agree to wait until tomorrow."

"I'll see to it that they make it as quick and painless as possible for him," Sarah said.

She nestled more closely against him. "He's so

young, Nick. You know, there's a very good chance
he won't remember any of this in a few years. And,
if he does, I'll be here to help him handle it. Your
aunt, by the way, already has us living on my parents' retirement property north of the city.''

He sighed again. ''Will you mind, my love, sharing a home with a wicked old gypsy until her time
runs out?''

Sarah shook her head and smiled. ''No more than
I'll mind sharing a home with the son of a pirate
who also happens to be a knight.''

''Did you say Leo was still asleep?'' he asked.

''I did. Did you say something about taking me to
bed?''

''I did indeed, my love.''

*   *   *   *   *

Next month, look for

UNDER THE KING'S COMMAND
(IM#1184)

by Ingrid Weaver when

ROMANCING THE CROWN

continues—only from
Silhouette Intimate Moments.
Here's a sneak preview...

How would it feel for a man to suddenly discover he was a father?

Like all Navy SEALs, Sam Coburn was accustomed to thinking on his feet, to adapting quickly to changes whenever he was on a mission, but his new assignment was rapidly taking more twists than the cobblestone streets he'd just navigated. He was supposed to be advising the Montebellan Police in their search for the woman who had murdered King Marcus Sebastiani's nephew, Desmond Caruso. It wasn't a typical assignment for a SEAL who was trained in counterterrorism, but King Marcus had wanted someone with an objective viewpoint, someone with a reputation for success.

With little more than an artist's sketch of the murderer to go on, the search would be challenging, to say the least. But Sam thrived on challenges. He had been in a strategy session with the king when the call from the hospital had come in.

An abandoned baby? A royal heir, the son of the recently restored Prince Lucas? The news was a shock to everyone. And from the information the hospital staff had relayed, the woman who had attempted to abandon the child apparently had proof of its parentage. Moreover, she had some connection with the murderer Sam was seeking. With the swift decisiveness that was typical of his leadership, the king had terminated the meeting. Rather than taking the time to form a convoy of palace staff and body-guards, he'd decided to commandeer Sam and his military jeep to take him, the queen and Prince Lucas to the hospital.

"Son?" Marcus laid his hand on Lucas's shoulder.

Lucas got out of the jeep, his movements stiff. He nodded to Sam to lead the way.

The hospital lobby was bustling with activity, yet a ripple of silence spread as people recognized the royal family. A portly man in a gray security guard's uniform hurried forward, his face flushed. "Your Highness," he said, bowing to each of the royals in turn. "This is such an honor."

"Where's the child?" Lucas asked. His voice was hoarse, as tightly controlled as his features.

"He's in the emergency ward." The guard gestured toward a corridor on their right. "The doctors are checking him."

"Where's the woman who tried to abandon the baby?" Sam asked.

"She says her name is Gretchen Hanson. We're holding her in the security office in the north wing."

"Good work," King Marcus said. "Lieutenant Coburn and I will want to question Hanson before you turn her over to the police, but first things first." He patted Queen Gwendolyn's hand and gave his son an encouraging nod. "Let's take a look at this baby."

It was easy to determine which examining room the child was in by the crowd of hospital staff who were gathered outside the door. The same ripple of quiet that had marked the royals' arrival in the hospital spread through the ward. Sam realized it wasn't awe, it was respectful affection. The Montebellan people genuinely cared about their monarch, and they all wanted to be part of the drama that was unfolding. As one, the crowd moved aside from the door.

In a circle of light, a trio of doctors was bending over an examining table. At first glance, the table appeared to be empty, but then Sam focused on the tiny form at the top. A baby was lying on its back, gurgling softly as it clutched the end of a stethoscope.

"Oh, my Lord." Queen Gwendolyn drew in a sharp breath. "Marcus, look."

The king stared at the baby. In silence, he slipped his arm around his wife's shoulders.

"Look at his hair, look at his eyes," Gwendolyn went on. "And that chin. Do you see it?"

"Yes, Gwen," he said softly, pulling her close to his side. "I see."

Sam studied the child for a minute, then moved his gaze to the prince. What the queen had meant was clear. Lucas and the child shared the same dark brown hair, the same blue eyes, even the identical stubborn chin. The resemblance was so strong, it was unmistakable. A DNA test would undoubtedly have to be performed, considering the importance of proving the royal heir's identity, but to anyone with eyes, the paternity was obvious.

Like a man in a trance, Lucas moved forward. If he noticed that the child on the table was a younger version of himself, he gave no indication. He was still holding on to the tight control he'd been exhibiting since they left the palace. "Is he all right? Is he healthy?"

One of the doctors stepped aside, allowing Lucas to reach the table. "Yes, Your Highness. We've done a thorough examination, and the infant appears to be in good health."

The child stopped gurgling and met Lucas's gaze

with a disconcerting solemnity. Then suddenly, the baby smiled.

Lucas closed his eyes and tipped back his head, inhaling unsteadily. He was silent for a moment, his shoulders shaking with emotions Sam couldn't begin to imagine. Finally, Lucas blinked and touched his fingertips to the baby's cheek. "Jess," he whispered. His eyes gleamed with tears. "You have Jessie's smile."

Sam still didn't know all the details about the prince's story, but he did know the man was mourning the death of the woman he loved. And now Lucas saw his lover in his child.

Love wasn't something that Sam thought much about. With the demands of his career and the danger each mission entailed, he didn't have the opportunity or the inclination for serious relationships.

At least, that was the excuse he'd always given himself. Except for that one time five years ago…

Without warning, an image rose in his memory. Long auburn hair, green eyes, the sound of laughter, of skin sliding over sun-warmed skin. The image was so vivid, he could swear he caught her scent.

Gardenias. Passionate and feminine.

And fleeting.

Sam rubbed his face, trying to concentrate on his duty.

"I want to thank you and the hospital staff for your diligence." King Marcus shook hands with each doctor. "My family and I are in your debt for your care of our newest member."

Evidently the king didn't need to wait for the test results to confirm what he saw, either. He had just publicly recognized the baby as a Sebastiani. Queen Gwendolyn was already at Lucas's side, her elegant features lit in a grandmotherly smile as she cooed over her grandson.

"I'd also like to speak with the person who found him," the king said. "I understand she was a navy officer?"

"Yes, Your Highness."

At the soft voice from the shadows in the corner of the room, Sam's mouth went dry. No, it wasn't possible. He had just been thinking of her, so he must be imagining her voice. How could she be here? Why now?

A woman moved into the pool of light, her jogging shoes padding quietly on the tile floor. A pair of running shorts bared her long legs. A black T-shirt molded her breasts and a gold chain with a tiny charm circled her throat. Her auburn hair was a short-cropped mass of finger-combed tufts.

It hadn't been his imagination, Sam thought. Somehow, she really was here.

When had she cut her hair? When had she taken up jogging? Did she still cry over old movies? Did she ever think of him when she was alone at night and the sound of the waves were like signs from the past?

Kate. *His* Kate. In the flesh, and close enough to smell.

And beautiful enough to make him want to forget the promise he'd made her five years ago.

INTIMATE MOMENTS™

presents:

Romancing the Crown

With the help of their powerful allies, the royal family of Montebello is determined to find their missing heir. But the search for the beloved prince is not without danger—or passion!

Available in November 2002:
UNDER THE KING'S COMMAND
by Ingrid Weaver (IM #1184)

A royal mission brought Navy SEAL Sam Coburn and Officer Kate Mulvaney together. Now their dangerous mission—and a love that never died—might just keep them together forever....

This exciting series continues throughout the year with these fabulous titles:

Available only from Silhouette Intimate Moments
at your favorite retail outlet.

Where love comes alive™

Visit Silhouette at www.eHarlequin.com

SIMRC11

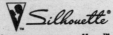

AVAILABLE IN OCTOBER FROM SILHOUETTE BOOKS!

THE
HEART'S COMMAND

THREE BRAND-NEW STORIES BY THREE
USA TODAY BESTSELLING AUTHORS!

RACHEL LEE
"The Dream Marine"

Marine sergeant Joe Yates came home to Conard County ready
to give up military life. Until spirited Diana Rutledge forced him
to remember the stuff true heroes—and true love—are made of….

MERLINE LOVELACE
"Undercover Operations"

She was the colonel's daughter, and he was the Special
Operations pilot who would do anything for her. But once
under deep cover as Danielle Flynn's husband, Jack Buchanan
battled hard to keep hold of his heart!

LINDSAY McKENNA
"To Love and Protect"

Reunited on a mission for Morgan Trayhern, lieutenants
Niall Ward and Brie Phillips found themselves stranded at sea—
with only each other to cling to. Would the power of love give
them the strength to carry on until rescue—and beyond?

Available at your favorite retail outlet.

Silhouette®
Where love comes alive™

Visit Silhouette at www.eHarlequin.com   PSTHC

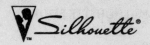
Silhouette®

COMING NEXT MONTH

INTIMATE MOMENTS™